MW01035096

OVER THE DARKENING FIELDS

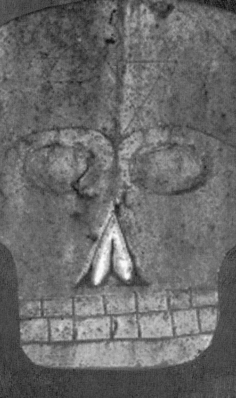

SCOTT THOMAS

DARK REGIONS PRESS
2007

SECOND EDITION

Text Copyright © 2007 by Scott Thomas

Cover and interior design by
David G. Barnett
Fat Cat Design

New Fiction:

The House of Murals
The August Ritual
Westermead Manifestation
Cabin 13
Thin Walls
Milton Crane's Collection
The Doll
The Virgin
Over the Darkening Fields
Hindenburg Kiss
The Wickhampton Bleeding
A Mishap and its Aftermath
The Nyssa
The Cinnamon Mask
The Sarah

Previously published fiction:

A Certain Gravity: appeared in *the kore*, Nov. 1994
Bag of Hell: *Pluto's Orchard*, Aug. 1998
Winter Census, *The Inflated Graveworm* (e-zine), Aug. 1998
The Storm Horses: appeared in *Flesh and Blood*, Feb. 2001
Three-legged Stool: *Terror Tales* Webzine, 2002
Halloween Tea: appeared in *Literary*, Jan. 1998
The Girl in the Attic: appeared in *Outer Darkness*, Jan. 2001
The Crippled Gate: appeared in *Thirteen Stories*, Oct. 2002
The September Fair: appeared in *Flesh and Blood*, Jan. 2000
Shadow Painting: appeared in *Shadowland*, April 1998
Julia's Fancy: appeared in Red Jack, Oct. 2002

ISBN: 978-1-62641-070-1

DARK REGIONS PRESS, LLC
6635 N. BALTIMORE AVE. STE 241
PORTLAND, OR 97203
DARKREGIONS.COM

CONTENTS

PART

—

ONE

THE HOUSE OF MURALS

Unremarkable, virtually invisible from the street, the house crouched grey in its cover of maples. While the trees had given up their leaves, they grew dense—old and young alike—in an inadvertent wall, an obscuring strata. The whole scene was conjured from November's dreary paint box—the house, the branches, the sky—even the predicted snow would show grey in the shadows of this place.

A man parked his car near the house and stood, evaluating it briefly before making his approach. He was in harmony with the essence of the environment, thin and forgotten-looking, his coat an inscrutable color, his pewter hair like shadows on snow.

A small cardboard box was held under one arm and the bones inside of it shifted as the man, a Mr. Benton, made his way up the steps to the door. He unlocked the house and entered.

Wan light did little to disclose the interior, the light itself as cool as the air. In short, the rooms were barren and neglected, the wooden floors scuffed, the corners webbed and the ceilings decayed, their slats showing like flattened brown ribs through wounds in the plaster.

The only features worthy of note were the cloth murals that draped the walls. Muddled by mildew, the distinguishable imagery was all but submerged in the very material that bore it. Medieval colors had soaked up the night dark of the rooms and, even on close inspection, Mr. Benton could not tell whether the art was the work of stitchery or paint.

Illustrations from a children's book for the denizens of hell, that's what Benton thought of the murals. The figures were stylized, elongated, practically whimsical in character and the animals stood upright, clad in incomplete suits of armor. But even the hares and horsies belied a sinister aspect—thin and bloodless, leering from behind their mildew drapes.

The lengths of cloth obscured the windows; weak November light offered a sickly radiance. It gave an undernourished glow to a blurry naked woman who hung from a tree by her hair, and made the scrawny dogs dangling alongside her seem compositions of birch.

Despite the chill, Mr. Benton's skin dampened beneath his clothing. He paced the perimeter of one of the first floor rooms, studying the musty art with the box under his arm and a penknife in his pocketed fist. He started at the sound of the box's contents shifting.

"I've brought the bones of a sparrow," Mr. Benton said at last.

《《—》》

November light belonged in the library as surely as Mr. Benton did. Dusk ushered the other humans away, relieving him of the task of externalization. He was left to his silence, his pages, his desk and its tea stains, the comfort of the musty air.

He made his rounds of the second and third floors before closing up. One set of footsteps, many, many books.

In the dimness and echoing marble of the lobby, Mr. Benton encountered the new assistant. Evelyn had an embarrassed smile when she turned, glancing up from a tall glass display case.

"I was just leaving," she said; her eyes lingered on him longer than he liked.

"I was about to leave, myself," Benton said. He hovered in the mouth of the stairwell.

Evelyn turned back to the case—she reflected in the glass, shy, pretty, plump, auburn hair on her shoulders. Dusty stuffed birds were ranked on shelves, their bases marked with tags of brittle yellow.

"They're lovely," Evelyn noted, "but it's so sad."

"Yes, ironic," Benton noticed. "I've always felt that taxidermy is something of a cruel art."

The woman studied him; for a moment she was Mona Lisa. Mr. Benton hoped it wasn't fondness in her gaze.

"Wasn't there a sparrow before?"

Benton blinked. "It was infested with insects, so I threw it away."

"Oh. Well, I better let you lock up. Good night, Mr. Benton."

He watched her walk away. She always borrowed a book to take home with her, he'd noted—he found that agreeable. Perhaps she had no one to go home to. While it was difficult for him to imagine a person *wanting* to go home to other humans, he felt something like a sadness for her.

The man muttered a farewell then locked the door behind Evelyn. He went to the display case and opened it. This time he took a small white owl. It was light in his hand—feathers and bones and two glass eyes.

«« — »»

Snow lent a false brightness to the outside of the house and gave the maples a stark, etched appearance. The flurries, as forecasted, had come with the dusk—a shattered whisper of white through the branches—a fine dust on the building's steps.

While the masses congregated over the corpses and wishbones of their holiday turkeys, Mr. Benton walked a solitary circle in the room of dank murals.

He no longer feared the place. He came here more and more often. Rather than deplete the library's display case of its birds, he had turned to other sources. Chickens from a butcher's shop, a goose as well. A pigeon found in a gutter, a crow from a parking lot.

«« — »»

Evelyn was taking too long with the returns, Mr. Benton thought. November had snowed its way into December and it was Christmas Eve. The others had left early, taken the nuisance of their cheer with them. Earlier Evelyn had asked if he had plans for the holiday. He had been evasive, sensing a possible invitation lurking behind her inquiry. Following the dictates of dreaded small talk, he had returned the question. Evelyn had said that she was going to stay at her apartment and re-read A CHRISTMAS CAROL.

Impatient now, Benton went looking for Evelyn. As it turned out, she was gone from the building, but when he returned to his desk, he found a small colorfully wrapped gift sitting on his desk. She must have waited for him to leave his station so as to deliver it unseen.

Following some hesitation, Benton took up the little box and carefully removed the wrapping from it, like a surgeon with his letter opener. Inside, tucked in a nest of soft, crinkled paper, he found a lovely blue glass paperweight in the shape of a bird. Mr. Benton smiled.

«« —»»

"I have brought the bones of a gull."

The murals looked all the more ancient in candlelight—the pigments from some distant dusty autumn, ground up and smeared in the darkness. Those illustrated figures not obliterated by stains peered fixedly from within their cloth internment—human and beast alike. They were brittle, as spare and encircling as the maples out in the snow.

Benton's voice echoed and the cloth rippled, breezes like veins pressing out behind the shadowy figures that lurked in the mildew. Meager and impossible, the shape of a body took form between the wall and the cloth, the tapestry accommodating as if a membrane.

With no sound to mark its progress, it slid along one wall, then the next until it had gone fully around the chamber. An arm's length from Mr. Benton, the shape pressed out more eagerly, the contours of a face straining against the hoary cloth.

Taking the penknife from his pocket, Mr. Benton stepped up to the wall. He cut a small hole in the spot where a mouth should have been. One by one he fed the delicate white bones into the hole—brittle wing bones, crooked claws, beak, neck and the rest. The darkness behind the jagged little opening sucked them in—cold breath on Benton's fingers.

«« —»»

He must have fallen asleep...Benton found himself in a strange place. He was in what appeared to be a dimly lit living room. There were two half-drunk mugs of chocolate (now gone cold) sitting on a coffee table in the glow of an evergreen-scented candle. A slim book by Dickens sat on the cushion beside him. He vaguely remembered someone reading to him from it. Other memories—half-formed murmurs—hovered just out of reach. He wondered if he had actually placed a phone call following his visit to the house of murals, or if the recollection was just the residue of a dream.

There were other books as well—the small rooms were marked by stacks of them, the bookcases crowded. Christmas songs were playing from a reproduction cathedral radio in the darkened kitchen, its cyclopean dial-light glowing orange. Benton walked quietly through the apartment.

He didn't remember killing her, but there was Evelyn, wide-eyed, naked, plump and pale, hanging from the curtain bar in the bathroom. She was hanging from her long auburn hair.

Too bad, he thought; she seemed a nice enough creature. He had actually begun to like her. Still, there was no use in abandoning an opportunity. Perhaps the murals were tiring of birds.

Mr. Benton opened his penknife and cut into the woman. His hand slipped inside her as if into a greased glove, groping for bones.

THE AUGUST RITUAL

Every August I go back to the cemetery, hoping to see something. People would think it strange if they saw me, lying on the hood of my car, propped against the windshield, gazing off into the night sky. My wife is starting to get used to the adventure, and I suspect she's growing fond of it, too. Someday I hope to have a child to bring, to share those fleeting streaks of meteor light.

It started with my Uncle John. He was a lovable sort; gray, gentle and good-humored. He never lost his sense of wonder and he urged me to appreciate the fine details of the world around me. Life was textures and smells and precarious temporary moments of magic around John.

Adventure was never far off when I was small and the world had yet to be demystified by the demands and concerns of adulthood; when I had the heart of a boy and was going to live forever. Back then the worst thing that could happen was school (worse than death, for that was too abstract, intangible).

John was a magnet to adventure, like the time we were driving past the reservoir and discovered a large snapping turtle sunning itself in the middle of the road. He stopped the car and got out, afraid that someone would come along and run over the poor beast. I climbed from the car and followed, hovering at a safe distance. The snapper's beaked head retracted—a prehistoric jack-in-the-box in reverse. Uncle John grabbed the creature's tail and dragged its hissing sage-colored bulk back into the grass that bordered the water.

Then there was the Sunday when we were hunting wild blueberries and a summer storm came pounding out of the west. We sheltered in a grove of maples at the edge of a field. The sky was gray fists and noise and the wind and rain shook the trees so hard that leaves fluttered about us like frightened birds. I dropped my bag of berries and grasped John's hand, my invincible boy heart having second thoughts about mortality, until I looked up and saw the quiet smile on the old man's face.

During the summers, back when I lived in Eastborough, I spent a good deal of time at the old fellow's place. He lived on the second floor of an old slate—blue Colonial beside the long tree—shaded entrance to the Catholic cemetery. There were few houses on the street—the residential section thinned, giving way to farmland. Though the busy center of town was little more than five minutes away, one had a sense of isolation.

I remember a number of occasions when my uncle talked about "*that sad—looking young man.*" Every once in a while, John would look down from his kitchen window and watch a tall gaunt man with morose features striding slowly out of the cemetery. It was invariably dusk. The fellow would travel the long paved path to where it met the street, then head off toward town. It was not uncommon for folks to stroll in the place—lots of people appreciate the gentle park-like quality some cemeteries have. Funny though, how John never saw the man entering the place; just leaving.

«« — »»

There was something mystical about venturing into the graveyard at night to watch for meteors. I remember the last time we went. It was mid-August, the time when the Earth was within viewing range of the Perseid meteor shower. There was a clammy chill in the air and a spicy scent of damp sod. September could not have been far away. Darkness transformed the place, melting the boundaries, blurring them into misty clots of trees. The familiar tar roads I knew so well by daylight were ethereal mottlings of shadow and moonlight. The headstones were indistinct and the place felt unnaturally spacious, open. Red lanterns, close to the ground, shone on marble monuments and blinked behind others. Distant trucks moaned along 495 as I clung to the comfort of Uncle John's big paw.

There was a grass rotary where a life—sized crucifixion statue loomed. I looked up at it as we passed, could just make out the scrawny limbs of a figure silhouetted against the moon's haze.

At the back of the cemetery there was a field that stretched off into the distance. An opalescent layer of localized ground fog made it seem as if the field itself were turning into vapor. We stood beneath dark trees, looking out at a quartz-dappled sky beside a lone wooden post where a fence had been. The fence was gone, and at that moment it seemed other borders were indistinct, ephemeral. My vibrant child's imagination convinced me that if I were to wade out into that damp moon—luminous mist, I would slip into a realm of unfamiliar intangibility.

"Look!" Uncle John said, pointing toward the horizon.

It was brief, a bronze smudge as debris burnt in the Earth's atmosphere. I clung to John's hand. The speed and brightness of the thing accentuated the strangeness of its silence.

I looked up at the man whose eyes were twinkling to defy the wrinkles. He wore a boyish smile.

Other meteors followed, rewarding our patience—fleeting streaks, slashing tails. While I did not conceptualize at the time, I had a curious fateful feeling about that night. There I stood, a young boy with an old man in a graveyard by that lone ruin of a fence…meteors darting briefly, dying silently.

«« —»»

Mrs. Bell was a nice middle-aged widow who owned the house where Uncle John lived. She was the last to see him, except for that sad-looking young fellow who held John's hand as they walked off into the cemetery one August dusk.

Every August I come back to watch the shooting stars slashing quietly above the misted field. It's something of a ritual. Sometimes I wonder what I'll see there in the dark. I wonder, I shiver and I smile.

THE VIRGIN

Molly Peterson came to my office following her first suicide attempt. A colleague of mine, who had tended to her at Saint Vincent's Hospital after her trip to the emergency room, had referred her to me.

She was a nervous woman, haggard, with mid-length brown hair and large distracted eyes. While she complained of suffering constant fatigue, there was restlessness about her.

My standard approach, when working with a new patient, is to start with childhood memories and progress up to the present, trying to get an overview, or spot significant events, or telltale patterns. Considering what she had done, I assumed that the woman had suffered some form of depression and I wanted to ascertain whether there was any abuse in her past.

"No one ever *touched* you?" I asked.

"No. No one ever touched me like *that*," she replied, somewhat indignant.

"No relatives? Someone at school, or a family friend?"

"No. No one has ever touched me in that way."

"I see. You've never been married?"

"No."

"Any lesbian experiences?"

"No!" Molly seemed horrified.

"Then I take it you're a virgin?"

"Yes." Molly smiled for the first time.

I proceeded to question her, ruling out any recollection of physical abuse, before focusing on the religious factor, which had reared up earlier in our conversation.

"You come from a Christian background?"

"I'm a Catholic," Molly said, defensively.

"You were raised Catholic?"

"Yes."

"You're practicing? You go to church?"

"Of course."

I pondered briefly, then said, "Molly, doesn't the Catholic Church consider suicide a sin?"

"Yes, it does."

"Yet you tried to kill yourself…"

Molly did not respond. She gazed about my office with dark eyes.

"Molly, have you tried to hurt yourself before?"

"No."

"Have you thought about killing yourself in the past?"

"I suppose. We all have at some time, I'd imagine. But I have my faith."

"It doesn't plague you then? When you're upset or you suffer a failure, you don't wish you could die?"

She looked in my eyes and shook her head.

I proceeded. "Did something happen to make you want to harm yourself?"

She nodded.

"Would you be able to tell me what that something was?"

"The Virgin," Molly said, "she came to me."

I scribbled notes and she watched me quietly.

"Molly, when you say The Virgin, you're referring to the Madonna, the Mother of God, according to your spiritual beliefs?"

"Yes. The Virgin Mother."

"Has she appeared to you more than once?"

"Mm hm. A number of times."

"When did you first see her?"

"When I turned thirty-five, last December."

"Where did this take place?"

"At the Pizza Pantry, where I work. I was alone in the building. I saw a figure in a long black robe slip into the ladies' room. I thought it was a nun. I went to the door and opened it, but there was no one there."

"Did you think it was The Virgin Mary at that time?"

"No, not yet."

"Tell me about the next time you saw her."

Molly drummed slender fingers on the arms of her chair, concentrating on me with her mournful eyes.

"It was a week or so later. I had done the grocery shopping and was putting things away. My mother was sick that night—usually we put the groceries away together, but she was up in bed. I had opened a box of tea; I get the tea that comes with a little porcelain animal tucked in the middle of the tea bags. I love looking to see which animal I'll discover; I collect them and keep them on the bureau in my room. I remember being disappointed because it was the mountain goat, and I already have that one, so I went and opened the cellar door to put it in a bag hanging on the wall at the top of the stairs, where I keep doubles. I give them to the Salvation Army shop so that poor children can have them.

"Well, I looked down the steps and saw a woman in a black hooded robe standing looking up at me."

"What did you feel at that time?"

"Shock."

"Did you recognize her?"

Molly shook her head. "No. It was dark and she sort of faded backward into the basement shadows."

"So you still had no idea that it was the Virgin Mary?"

"Not at that point. Not until the next time."

I sat back. "Tell me about it."

"It was after work one night, and I felt dirty after getting grease and tomato sauce on my clothes. I turned on the shower to let the water get warm, then shut the curtain. It's an old house and it takes a while for the water to heat up. I waited until I saw steam coming up then I took off my clothes and opened the curtain. She was standing there with the water spraying through her, looking right at me...."

Molly put a hand to her chest and sighed.

I said, "You recognized her?"

"Oh, yes. It was The Virgin—who else could it have been? It was a vision, a miracle."

"How long did you see this vision for, Molly?"

"Several seconds, I guess. Long seconds. I just stood there in awe, as you can imagine."

"Yes."

"Then she spoke to me."

I sat forward, intrigued. "You heard her speak?"

"Oh, yes. She said 'I love you, Molly. I'm waiting for you.'"

"Was that all?"

Molly nodded, dragging squeaky fingertips on the leather arms of the chair. "Then she faded into the steam, and I knelt down to pray."

I doodled a cross on my notepad.

"Tell me more, Molly; what do you think she meant by saying that she was waiting for you?"

"She meant that she was waiting for me in Heaven."

"Do you hear voices at times, other than when you see these images?"

"No. I'm not crazy, you know. I didn't imagine it. She spoke to me."

"I understand. Has she spoken to you since the time in the shower?"

"Yes."

"What happened?"

"It was a month later. I woke up in the middle of the night and she was standing on my chest staring down at me. It was strange, because she had no weight, yet she was standing on me.

"It was dark, but I could see how lovely she was. Her skin was white like porcelain; there was no color in her face, except for her black eyes, and her tongue. It was very red, bloody looking.

"I was speechless, like before, but she smiled and she spoke in the most soothing soft voice. I felt so calm, calmer than I've ever felt before."

"She said 'I love you, Molly. I want you to come with me. I want you to put your rosary beads down your throat and die.'"

I shuddered.

"Then she was gone."

"So," I said, clearing my voice, "she suggested that you commit suicide—which, as I pointed out, is a contradiction in terms of what the Church proclaims?"

"Under normal circumstances, but this was The Virgin Mother..."

"So, she was giving you special license?"

"Yes."

"And you were not depressed at the time?"

"Oh, no. I was exhilarated."

"That's when you put the necklace in your throat?"

"Mm hm. I put it in my mouth and tried to swallow it. I began to choke and then I passed out."

"I understand your mother found you and called for help."

Molly looked sad. "She ruined it."

"So, you want to die?"

She looked at me as if I had said something absurd.

"The Virgin wants me."

《《——》》

I prescribed a prozac-class antidepressant and pherphenazine, an anti-psychotic drug, for Molly Peterson and made an appointment for her to see me the following week.

Molly had resisted my insistent suggestions that she spend some time in a psychiatric hospital, and frankly, I was concerned about her. I called each day to see how she was and each time I was relieved to hear that the delusional visitor had not reappeared.

《《——》》

I was awakened one night by a shrill sound, which turned out to be the phone. I had rolled over, half-conscious, and felt a figure beside me on the bed. My hand landed on someone's open mouth. I felt lips and teeth and groped up higher where there was only softness like jelly.

Startled, I pulled my hand away and turned a light on. I was alone in the bed. I picked up the phone; it was my doctor friend from Saint Vincent's Hospital calling to tell me that Molly Peterson had committed suicide. She had gone up into the attic at her family home, taken one of her deceased father's old shotguns and fired it into her face, removing much of her head from the nose up.

《《——》》

I paid a visit to Molly's mother following the funeral. She was a gentle old woman, and she offered me tea and the opportunity to view her daughter's room. I felt sad standing there looking at the prized collection of small glossy animals lovingly arranged on the bureau. One shape seemed to stand out.

"It came in the tea, the night she did it," Mrs. Peterson said.

I picked up the glistening black porcelain image of a solemn woman in a long hooded robe.

"That's strange," I noted.

"Must've gotten in by mistake," Mrs. Peterson speculated. I agreed.

I realize that the actions that followed will seem unprofessional, but I could not resist the impulse, or ignore the curious feeling of dread that filled me upon coming into contact with the figurine... I slipped the thing into my pocket when Mrs. Peterson wasn't looking. After I left, I stopped at the nearest stretch of secluded road and smashed the little black horror on the pavement.

WESTERMEAD MANIFESTATION

One of my patients, a 50-year old automobile mechanic, came to my office on May 1st, 1999 with an injury. Martin Keller's left forearm bore a curious disfigurement, reportedly the source of notable chronic pain. I examined the three black parallel lines, but failed to determine what had caused them. The damage was inconsistent with conventional burning or even with chemical burns. The patient's explanation led me to believe that he was suffering from some form of mental disorder and had deliberately caused harm to himself.

Keller claimed that he had traveled (by what means was not clear to him) to a primitive village in a place he called Westermead. There, he encountered a lady in a cloak wearing a metal mask. The mask swung open and out sprang a flailing mass of black tendrils, which grasped at his arm before he fled. He suffered severe burning sensations on his arm. I referred the patient to a psychiatrist and a dermatologist and did not see him again.

The following August, I attended a conference where a colleague mentioned a remarkable case he had witnessed in Japan during the summer of 1992. A young man spontaneously acquired roof-thatching skills and claimed that he bodily transported to a distant land called Westermead. He described the place in great detail, claiming that it was a massive island, a beautiful, mystical place of quaint villages and wild expanses. Technologically speaking, this distant land was comparable to our late 1600s.

Mr. Musashi's doctor determined that he was suffering delusions and suggested that he seek therapy. The patient refused, but returned some weeks later. This time Mr. Musashi complained that a highwayman had fired a musket at him as he was transporting back into his home dimension. X-rays determined that there was, indeed, some kind of foreign mass embedded in the patient's right thigh. Surgery revealed this mass to be a small musket ball. There was no damage to suggest a point of entry; it was as if it had simply appeared there in the muscle.

There have been twelve other cases that I am aware of. Most of the patients exhibited behavioral rather than physical symptoms, for instance, cooking foods native to this alleged Westermead—recipes like fenberry scones and treacle hooves (a form of molasses pastry). Others spoke in a Westermead accent (British sounding, it seems) and sang songs about a North War and seasonal celebrations. One patient, believing that she had become a Spell woman, conjured a localized rain shower over her condominium in Newport, Rhode Island.

Interviews with the patients revealed that their excursions occurred sporadically, usually during quiet moments and invariably when they were alone. None reported any episodes while driving automobiles, fortunately. All maintained that they were physically displaced and that their visits averaged in length between ten minutes and two hours. The sensation of journeying to and from Westermead has been described as a feeling of fading, accompanied by confusion and tingling of the limbs.

I conducted an experiment with Maxine Prior, the patient from Rhode Island. I spent hours with her, waiting to observe her during one of her otherworldly visits. All attempts proved fruitless. She said that it would not happen when I was present, so I set up a video camera to monitor her over a period of weeks. Each night she would spend several hours in a reclining chair with the camera running. On the 22nd day, Ms. Prior had a Westermead episode, but whether or not she physically dematerialized could not be determined. The camera taped only what appeared to be a blizzard, but when examined by audio-visual experts at Boston University, seemed to show a continuous slow motion storm of apple blossom petals. This went on for close to two hours and at one point on the tape, one could hear what sounded to be distant fiddle music and laughter.

The one fatal case that I am aware of concerned a 44 year-old

Mexican man, who was detained by authorities as an illegal alien in Texas. The man spoke only Spanish, until one night when he started describing a village called Brinkers Down, on the River Sour, Westermead. He spoke eloquent English with a British accent, according to his jailers. The patient claimed that he was ill with the Goat Plague and soon fell into a coma. Several days later, the man woke from his coma, sprang from his bed, danced about maniacally and proceeded to explode. The authorities theorized that the man must have been smuggling some drug-related chemicals, swallowed in balloons. The ensuing postmortem (difficult due to the fractured state of the body) revealed no evidence to support that theory, but it did show findings of an undigested mushroom of an unknown species.

I have found no common correlation between the patients. There seems to be no pattern in terms of race, age, sex, socio-ecological background or education. The only apparent link is the consistency of their experiences, ie: their descriptions of the elusive Westermead.

A small personal note: I have sampled a barley brew made from an old Thistlekeep (a town in the Westermead Midlands, Im told) recipe. It is finer than any ale that this dimension has to offer.

BAG

OF

HELL

When old Tyler finished raking the leaves for his neighbor, he marched up onto the porch and knelt beside the faded young woman seated in a rocking chair.

"So, Emma, how's your baby boy?" Tyler asked.

Emma stared across the lawn into the grey wood beyond.

Tyler lit a cigarette.

"Did they find out what that tumor-thing was?" the man asked, squinting as he exhaled smoke.

"A bag of hell," Emma stated numbly.

"Excuse me?"

"I cut it out. It's in the kitchen sink right now. Listen, you can hear it growling…"

Tyler shifted uncomfortably. He looked to the screen door and the dim room behind it, straining to hear. He was not sure whether that was or was not growling coming from the kitchen.

"You mean your boy's dead?"

Emma nodded and pointed to the woods.

"I put him out there," the woman said.

Tyler strained his old eyes but saw only the tangled strata of branches and the fluttering black of agitated crows and something like a wasp's nest, bloated and grey, high in the leafless limbs.

They were quiet for a time. The wind came and a rocker creaked and something like drowning thunder sounded behind the screen door.

"Would you care to stay for dinner, Tyler?" Emma said, at last. "I made some nice hot soup. Hotter than hell."

Tyler scrunched his cigarette out on the battered porch and rose, tipping his cap.

"Ahh, no thank you, Emma; I think I'd better be getting home to feed the dogs."

The man moved quickly to the path that led him away from Emma's house. He resisted the urge to look back and lit another cigarette with trembling hands.

The hungry voices of crows echoed in the darkening wood.

THE STORM HORSES

When Riane learned she was dying, she went to Sesqua Valley. She found a thin tree in the fat shadow of the twin mountains which perched above like great petrified wings. She ran her fingers over the lower branches, feeling for whispers. She made her choice and, exchanging a small red libation from a slice in her palm, cut free a branch. The following day she returned to her home in Innsmouth, Massachusetts.

《《——》》

It was a steep old house, the color of a rain-fed Atlantic, seated on a hill above a meadow. The bottom floor contained a potter's shop and dusky paintings and strange creatures fashioned from painful twists of driftwood. The branch waited downstairs until the moon came up from the sea, abandoned in the sky like a shell on a beach.

Riane tied back her long light hair, burned incense, removed her clothing, walked down the slow stairs. The branch leaned in a corner, pulsing with Sesqua darkness. Candles were lit and tools readied, then Riane sat upon a stool with the branch across her legs, and set to work.

The dying woman shaped the branch into a staff—white, smooth, bearing at its top the head of a horse. The moon spun above the house, dimmed, descended westward as dawn made pink insinuations and, impatient, forced light onto the old sea-colored house. Trembling and chill in her nakedness, Riane collapsed, exhausted, to the shaving-strewn floor.

Later that morning, Lauren came to the house and found her sister; she helped her up to bed. Riane was too weak to go downstairs; her potter's wheel stood silent, her tubes of paint faded under dust, her carving tools never again to know the warmth of her hands.

The nights belonged to fever. Riane tossed in her sweat, told strange stories in her sleep, made a curious alphabet of gestures with hypnogogic fingers. Lauren sat by the bed throughout, watching as death's slow-sculpting hands shaped her sister into something fearful and sad.

«« — »»

One night Riane freed herself from the bed. It had been a month since the moon rose dripping from the Atlantic. She moved past her sister who slumped sleeping in a chair, left her guarding an empty bed and moved quietly to the first floor where the staff waited.

She walked out into the soft light. She walked down the hill, into the meadow behind the house. The wind shared a secret of wild herbs and brine. She tapped the earth with the staff as if to wake a heart beneath the field. The staff thundered in the ant mazes below and echoed in the air, where clouds wrapped the moon. Lightning thorned the sky.

A bolt found the staff, knocking it to the ground, burning it into the meadow.

«« — »»

The fevers were gone. Sleep seemed friendly enough; no more half-coherent mutterings, no more gnarled gesticulations. Riane grew thin and pale, her few spoken words like a mist. Lauren flitted between relief and terror, the lone witness to the process. The world had become a queer place as of late...

Lauren had seen the strange horse-shaped pattern of ashen white in the middle of the field, had seen lightning dance in the field and the pale horses that thundered about in the rain. How strange that they always vanished when the storms faded. How strange that the crows that pecked the horse-shaped mark turned white and hovered above it like gulls.

The night smelled like rain; Riane sat up in bed and stared at her sister. She told Lauren to go to the meadow and to bring her some of the dust from the place where lightning had fallen. Lauren assumed that the fevers were back, but her sister insisted, so she went.

Thunder mumbled in the distance and something snorted in the close darkness when Lauren bent to dig at the chalk-white horse. She hurried back to the steep house and up the stairs to her sister's room.

Riane smiled sweetly and whispered goodbye. She took the ash, touched it to her tears and died. Lauren held her hand until it went cold. Thunder stampeded across the meadow and wind flung the doors wide. Rainy white horses danced into the room, gathered about the bed and, grasping Riane's nightgown in square teeth, carried her limp body down the stairs, down the hill and into the field.

Lauren watched from the window as they dragged her limp and flopping sister about the wild grass, lightning spitting, rain hissing. White crows swirled above, calling, and Riane's legs stirred, flexed from under her soggy garment. The horses ran, skimming her feet over the damp earth until her feet stepped of their own accord and she was upright, moving. The horses released her and she ran, laughing in the grey brine of the air, her mane behind her in the galloping storm.

A CERTAIN GRAVITY

Jane Doyle studied her reflection in the plate glass window of the doughnut shop. It was pale, translucent. Cars stirred in the parking lot beyond—headlights flashing, break lights blinking red as people emptied from the adjacent theater and headed home. Jane barely noticed the commotion, her thoughts tangled in insecurities. She was constantly assessing herself, wondering how others perceived her exterior, the fleshy vehicle that carried her conscious about day to day. Now her own blank face stared back from the glass, like a store mannequin, or one of those waxen milk carton kids.

"We close in ten minutes, lady," the teenage boy behind the counter said.

Jane blinked. "Oh, okay." She hated being called 'lady.'

She gulped the last of her coffee and fumbled a tip onto the counter before rushing to the ladies room. She went to the mirror and launched into her ritual of checking mascara, rouge and lipstick. Moderation was the key to maintaining the mask. Too much looked cheap, not enough and her age showed. At thirty-eight she could not silence the signs of age, but at least she could keep them at a whisper.

This is crazy, she thought; *who's going to see me now, at midnight? The kid behind the register? Lord forbid I should get pulled over by a cop and have a mascara blob on my lashes.* She smirked ironically, even as she checked her hair and adjusted the collar of her shirt. Hair spray hissed.

She was attractive, her hair medium-length, professional-looking, with just enough waviness to conform to present standards of sexiness. Her body was holding up well after having two kids. She had even noticed the counter boy stealing a few cleavage peeks. There were times when it disgusted her to be measured and mentally stripped by leering gargoyles, yet she dreaded the day when men wouldn't care to look.

"Oh, shit!"

One of Jane's contact lenses popped out and fell into the sink.

Three raps on the door. "Five minutes, lady."

"Yeah, okay, I know!" She bent over the sink, garish phosphorescent light washing across the porcelain. "Where is it?"

There—it hadn't reached the drain opening. She pinned it with her index nail.

"Gotcha!"

«« —»»

The parking lot seemed bigger at night. Jane's white two-door sat alone. The flat blackness outside the shopping center stretched beyond the reach of the pole-lights. American suburbia slept in the distance.

The woman clacked across the pavement, reached into her purse and scrounged for the familiar jangling cool of keys.

"Oh, come on...

Jane peered in through the driver-side window and saw her keychain dangling from the ignition.

"Damn it!"

She hurried around to the passenger door and tried it, even though she knew it too would be locked.

"Oh, this is lovely."

Jane jogged back toward the doughnut place, her heels too loud, accentuating the quiet by contrast. She tried the door, which was locked. She went to the window, spotted the kid wiping down the counter and rapped on the glass. The kid looked up and frowned.

Jane mouthed the words: *I'm locked out of my car!* The kid shrugged and shook his head; he did not comprehend. Jane pointed out at her car; it sat alone in the humming pink haze of a lamp. Now the kid nodded and he came to meet her at the door.

Jane was nearly hyperventilating when the teen let her in.

"Oh, thanks! Do you have a pay phone?"

The kid pointed. "There. But my ride will be here in a few minutes…"

"I'll hurry." Jane hurried. She dialed her house, tapping her foot as she fished a cigarette out and lit it with a trembling hand. The phone rang several times on the other end then clicked. Her own voice came on, distant, metallic, bland.

"Hi. We can't come to the phone right now. Please leave a message after the beep and we'll get back to you." Beep.

Jane hissed smoke into the mouthpiece. "Brad! Pick up the phone. Brad, are you there, it's me. I'm locked out of my freaking car!"

She heard a clatter and a man's voice grumbled, "You're *what*?"

"I locked my keys in the car."

"That was stupid."

"Tell me about it. Look, can you bring down the spare?"

"Wait, where are you?"

"I'm at Eastboro Village, off route nine."

Brad groaned. "What are you doing there?"

"Brad, I've had a lousy day; don't start, please…I'm in no mood. The computers were down half the day and I had to stay late to straighten things out because they have some moron trainee there who doesn't know her asshole from her elbow. I stopped for a coffee so I can stay awake driving home, alright? So, are you coming?"

Brad gave the sigh he always used to make her feel foolish or guilty and muttered, "Yeah, I'm on my way." Click.

Jane sneered at the phone and hung up. "Jerk!"

《《—》》

Five minutes later a car pulled up outside the donut shop. The teen had gone against regulations and let Jane stay inside after closing time. He hadn't wanted to make a woman stand out in a parking lot alone after midnight, but now he was forced to do just that. Jane waited in the chill air as he locked the plate glass door.

The kid's father, a pulpy middle-aged man, sat gawking greedily from his idling vehicle. He looked her up and down, weighing, measuring, mentally peeling away her sexy-enough but dignified grey skirt suit. Jane sneered and looked off across the parking lot to where a distant highway hissed.

"Good luck," the kid said, getting into the car.

"Thanks."

They drove off. Jane watched the tail lights fade into blackness. Suddenly she felt terribly alone, horribly anonymous. Even if that kid's father was a creep, she'd have felt better having some form of human company. A certain gravity gripped her stomach and the coffee inside burned.

«« — »»

The wind had picked up. Newspaper pages hissed and skidded across the black pavement. Jane sought shelter in front of a shoe store where the doors were recessed and flanked by display windows. This offered her some semblance of cover, on three sides anyway. She paced, smoking, staring in at all those empty shoes, the frozen march of fleeting fashions. There was everything from hundred dollar walking shoes (glorified sneakers) to blood red pumps. Empty vessels waiting for the warmth of consumer's feet.

It had been fifteen minutes since she had called Brad. It was not quite a half hour's drive from their house to the shopping center. She was nervous. News reports of women being raped and murdered were all too common. People vanished all the time. What if some man were to drive up and see her standing there alone? Who would hear her scream?

"Come on, Brad…"

She poked out from the semi-enclosing glass display of footwear. A smirking dummy in a sports coat peered from the window of a men's clothing store next door. Jane started at the sight, her mind a whirl of agitation. She ducked back, hugging herself.

"Well, it's been quite a day, Jane, hasn't it?" she asked herself cynically. Some days it seemed as if there were snickering little fate gods perched in the ether gaining amusement from human frustration. Growing fat on frustration. She could almost sense their laughter at times, when things went wrong. It was really only a half-hearted speculation though, for Jane was far from convinced that there was such a thing as fate, or gods, or anything beyond the malls and condos, the food chains and televisions and fad-medicines modern Americans clung to. She even thought that religions were like make-up painted on the big bad unknown to give it a recognizable face. The practical part of her insisted that things happened arbitrarily…a bad day did not prove that a mean-spirited consciousness was manipulating things.

Jane gazed at her reflection superimposed over the ranks of vacant shoes. A wraith stared back with vague eyes, the lipstick a faint blur, the cheeks rouged with shadows. She reached automatically to adjust a strand of hair. The hair spray had made it feel brittle; it left grit on her fingers.

She leaned closer. Even in the dimness she could see the fear and desperation that usually nested repressed inside. Now, with her nerves on fire, these forces reared. An aging face cowered behind the make-up. Gravity would take her breasts and flatten them, draw at her buttocks, despite the futile aerobic gestures. Already there were bags weighing beneath her eyes, and her belly was starting to sag.

Age was another facet of the big bad unknown. Life out of control. She hid from her fear of it, burying herself in numbness and distraction, routine, until she almost forgot who she was. Some days she felt like a zombie, driving to work with that painted mask, fueling the machine with cigarettes and caffeine, safe beneath her helmet of hair spray. Some days she *became* the suits she saved to buy, the stylish shoes, the right perfume imprinting her on reality. She was only the movies she rented, only the foods she ate, only the latest radio hits, a ghostly reflection of the people who populated TV commercials. Oh, but they were young, and those nasty gods of gravity and time were sucking at the entropic flesh around her bones. She felt empty.

"It's been a day, Jane." Her voice had a tense shrillness.

The day played back in her mind…an alarm clock buzzing, Brad atop her briefly as if she were a blow-up doll, coffee hot in her hollow belly, a rabid toothpaste sneer, kids spilling milk across a table, traffic, computer screens, coffee, mirrors where she sprayed her hair and smoothed her face with smears of color. But she had *looked* composed, despite it all, until this moment.

"*Where is he?*" Jane spun away from the glass and looked out across the parking lot. The night sky was huge. A chill breeze swept down, a Styrofoam cup danced. Faded newspapers, half-drowned in a puddle, fluttered like a crippled gull.

"Come on, Brad, please…"

Jane felt heavy and exhausted. Her muscles ached. She reached down to rub at the back of her leg, shifting her weight to the other.

"Oh, crap!"

A run in her stocking.

She laughed. "Why not? Hey, everything else has gone to hell today—what's a little stocking run?"

She fingered the finely meshed material and the thin etched line.

"What the…"

Jane's hand drew back. She turned to catch the light better, bending for a closer view. At first she thought it was a varicose vein, which was horrifying enough, but then she realized it was a crack *beneath* the nylon. A crack in her leg.

"Oh, my God!"

Jane turned toward her car and started to run, stepping off the sidewalk that fronted the stores. Her ankle broke into crisp shards like pieces of crockery and clattered behind her. Gasping, she hobbled along. She groped at the darkness, shrieking as she saw her fingers tumble off and shatter on the ground as if brittle Christmas ornaments. She was only yards from the car…her left leg had broken away to the knee. She went down, the right arm snapping, flaking, scattering to the elbow. Groaning, she struggled upright, pushing onward.

"Help me!"

Her intact leg smashed as her weight came down on it, jaggy cracks snaking up to her hip. An ear fell like a fragile seashell, her eyelids like porcelain moths.

"Help!"

The car was close; she could see her fractured reflection tripping along in the window. She fell, her breasts breaking like teacups, her arms reduced to skittering chunks, the pieces breaking smaller as they rolled until they were dust. Jane lay there looking up at the car, at the ghostly reflection-like image of herself sitting behind the wheel.

As the rest of Jane crumbled into a sugary mist, the car drove off into the night.

《《——》》

Brad pulled up outside the donut shop and parked. He looked in the windows—it was dark inside with only the safety lights on, and there was no sign of Jane. Where was her car?

"Jane?" His voice echoed across the parking lot.

He heard a hollow clattering sound and turned. It was only an empty cup being rolled by the wind, but there was something else on the ground that caught his eye. Brad jogged over. Puzzled, he stared down at Jane's empty shoes.

THREE-LEGGED STOOL

Alastair Nolan loved his family tree, its tangled roots surging with fey Celtic sap, extending across the Atlantic to Ireland, Scotland and Wales, lands his fierce and poetic ancestry had called home. While he leaned an impassioned ear to Celtic pipes and harps, and delighted in the ambery barley brews that made their way across the Atlantic, it was the Celtic folklore that spoke to something deep within him, stirred the peat-fires that burned like archetypes in his DNA. Tales of magic, and other-worldly creatures, both mischievous and mysterious. Creatures beautiful and terrifying, enchanting, haunting.

Alastair was a walking bestiary, ever ready, at the slightest provocation, to offer a colorful discourse on wondrous horse-shaped phoukas, or the eerie lights called corpse candles, known to guide the unweary to watery sleep in ancient marshes, or the Daoine Sidh, the fairy folk that dwelt and danced within green and hollow hills. They filled the pages of the books piled in the dusty corners of his lonely room and they filled his imagination too, especially when he had spent too much time and money at Pickle's Pub, as was the case tonight.

《《—》》

Alastair staggered out to his rust-colored Buick and peeled the damp streamers of toilet paper (pseudo ectoplasm?) off the windshield.

Halloween pranksters, no doubt, either that or some of his drinking companions. He drove north, then east, then north again until the main road thinned and the night was a tunnel of lacy moonlight and emaciated trees. It was a perfect night for ritual, Halloween being a Celtic invention. Samhain they'd called it, when the material world waltzed with the non.

Humming Carolan's Farewell to Music, Alastair turned his car into the entrance of the state forest. The car heater rasped, attempting to fend off the encroaching cold. The road became dirt and the vehicle jostled, creaking like a haunted ship on a cold October sea. He had to find the spot where three roads converged.

The idea had come to him some weeks previous, when his dear mother had fallen in her bathroom at the retirement home. She had lain on the floor nearly an hour; the stroke, like some ingeniously malicious little night dweller, had pinched off her ability to cry for help. She had not been right since and Alastair was worried; Mum, his books and the creaking Buick were all he had left, following his divorce and the layoffs at the mill. Was she going to die?

Earlier that day Alastair had taken what was left of his unemployment check and driven to a discount furniture outlet, determined and anxious. Waiting to pay for his purchase, he had gazed out through large plate glass windows as the afternoon sky rotated westward; the sky expanded, became orange, grew chilly and watery. Birds went up like flecks of ash from a fire.

The headlights took him through the damp air, over leaf-paved roads until he came to the place he had been searching for. The road branched into three, each fading into tree-lined darkness. His books had told him about such places, how in old Scotland a man could sit where three roads met, on a three-legged stool and listen to the whispering of fairies and learn the names of those destined to die within the year. Alastair parked, climbed out of the car and, wobbling, walked behind it to open the trunk. A three-legged stool stood in musty darkness.

«« — »»

Alastair sat where three roads met, shivering, hunched, making ghosts with his breath, listening as his car engine cooled, creaking. The surrounding woods were full of breezes and dead leaves and the moon put frosty hands on everything. Long minutes passed and Alastair, swaying as gravity tempted him this way and that, listened closely when a steady hissing came from the dark behind him. He clenched his body around the quiet heat of his heart as shivers found his spine; at length he gathered the courage to turn, discovering the source of the noise. It was the Buick, its weight settling, the four tires deflating before his eyes. It seemed the Halloween pranksters had done more to the car than drape it with toilet paper.

"Lovely," Alastair muttered.

《《—》》

Sometime after midnight, with Alastair a few internal paces from sleep, with the cold tightening about his bulk, a voice came sighing out of the night.

"Willie Jackson," the voice seemed to say.

"Willie Jackson!" Alastair repeated, Willie being one of his drinking buddies. "Oh, no, not Willie."

Alastair removed his winter jacket and tossed it into the darkness; it was customary, according to lore, to placate the fairies with an article of clothing in order to spare those whose names were whispered. Willie was worth a coat. Alastair heard the garment thump on the dirt road and listened as it was dragged away, rasping over frosty leaves.

Something flitted in the dark, a huge moth it seemed, and the wind came closer, scented with October, and it spoke, "Jimmy Paulsen."

"Aww, not Jimmy!" Off went Alastair's left shoe.

More breezes brought more names…

"Lenny French." (Drinking buddy). Right shoe.

"George and Nettie Harrison." (Another drinking buddy and his wife). The socks went.

"Ed Trent."

Alastair, trembling, hugging himself asked, "Who's that?"

The night replied, "Your mail man."

"Oh." Off came the trousers.

《《—》》

It was late and cold and Alastair sat in his boxers on a three-legged stool with the night pooled about him. The vague winged thing was fluttering in the moon-chilled trees, its eyes like beads of ice. He waited to see who else was scheduled to die. He waited and waited until, at last the air stirred and a voice like frost hissed, "Your Mum!"

"No! No, damn it!" Alastair stood, tore off his boxers and tossed them into the dark. The wind took them, sighing.

The breeze paused, then came again. "*You,*" it said.

Alastair looked down at himself. He was naked.

«« — »»

They found Alastair the next morning, sitting in his Buick, frozen dead.

CABIN
13

The mountains appeared gradually, misty blue behemoths rising up behind the monotonous pines. The couple in the car was getting closer to their destination and there was so much behind them now—their home, their jobs, the congesting suburbia of central Massachusetts, ten years of marriage. The mountains were something of a prize, great rearing word balloons that might have been welcoming them to Down East, Maine, congratulating them for having survived the long trek of highway, the redundant beauty of the pines, the yuppies that drove as if ravenous, the locals who drove like demons.

Much had changed and much was the same since last they'd come to this part of the world. Maine was virtually another planet, its wilderness sprawling and grand. Not since their honeymoon, ten years back, had they seen any place like it. It was as if they were traveling back in time.

"There's that old farmhouse with the bear!" Sandra said.

The bear had been carved from the stump of a tree. It stood hunched and dark against the subtly colored scrub foliage of early September.

"I remember that," Paul said.

A man and his wife, camping somewhere in the western part of the country, had unfortunately encountered black bears some weeks back. Paul had heard about it on the radio. The man had briefly left the campsite for some reason or other, only to return and find two of the bulky dark mammals hovering over the red, twisted body of his wife. She had made the mistake of trying to run, had made the terrible mistake of bleeding to death.

"They have black bears up here," Paul said, nonchalantly.

Sandra grinned. "I know." She hadn't heard that news story.

More familiar landmarks came, now that they were off the highway. There were houses and farms spread out along the seemingly endless roads; antique shops, lobster pounds, homey restaurants, gift stores, inns, motels, campgrounds.

Six hours in the car, minus the time spent at rest stops, had filled Paul with an older person's skeleton.

"Wouldn't it be nice if there were a Jacuzzi and a chiropractor waiting at our cabin?" Paul joked.

"That's not very rustic, Paul." Sandra did not sound entirely amused.

"My bones are rustic."

The smell of the sea came into the car and the shadow of a hawk flitted over the road. They caught glimpses of the bay through the trees on the right, sudden rocky coves, surreal life-sized postcards. The water was calm in afternoon light.

A sign announced Landor's Bay Cabins and the car, at last, pulled off the road, crackling over the gravel outside of a weathered barn. A slim woman with a look reminiscent of a Native American came out of the small adjacent office, smiling.

"The honeymooners! You made it!"

There were smiles and hugs and small talk. Linda, the dark-haired woman, and her husband Dan, had been operating the site for years, had been running it ten years back when Sandra and Paul had honeymooned in cabin 13.

The pines had just dragged the sun down when the couple drove away from the office and the antique shop that Linda ran out of the attached barn. Rocks popped beneath the tires along the dirt road that wound through a scrubby meadow of hinting russet and wildflowers. Along one side of the property, facing the breezy openess of grass and brush, stood thirteen box-like shingled cabins. They were lined up like a child's blocks, over where the dirt road led and ended.

"I can't believe we're here again," Sandra said excitedly.

"Me too!" Paul smiled.

"Look, there's our cabin!" Sandra took Paul's hand.

46

《《——》》

The cabin was a museum of sorts, the furnishings a quirky mix of odd bits from various periods. The windowed sun room held an old 1950s table set and twin, curiously streamlined chairs from the 60s. An older two-tiered table sat between those, between the two side windows that looked out on the bay. In the dark, cramped main chamber, the bed was a creaky blob of white in a corner. There was a small gas stove and shelves and a tiny offering of counter space. A window over the sink faced more meadow, its vegetation taller and wilder, the high yarrow still capped in gold, stalks clumped like cages around shadow, touches of early autumn on leaves in prudent red and cautious yellow.

Not only was cabin 13 cozy and haunted by the feel and scent of ocean air, it was full of memories, their own and those of strangers. Other couples, other lovers had slept there and the eclectic furniture, collected from estate sales largely, had known the warmth of those who now were likely dead.

Candlelight agreed with the place, made fidgeting stars of the bubbles in their glasses of champagne. It made their faces softer-looking, warmer, while alternately hiding their eyes. They ate at the table in the closed-in sun room, a quick pasta meal Sandra had made in the kitchen corner of the cabin.

After the pasta, after the champagne, they went to bed. While neither could remember the last time they had been naked together, they made love as if young and meadow-wild.

《《——》》

Cabin 13 stood closest to the bay, its side windows offering the finest view. The mostly-broken shell of an oak, deceivingly greened by parasitic vines, stood starkly against the placid water. An undulating sprawl of brush and grasses, tall spiky sea roses pouting red hips like Christmas ornaments, separated number 13 from a steep ridge where pines tried to balance, close by the rock-strewn shore. But Paul could not, from his window vantage point, see where the shore actually met the Atlantic, for the steep grassy land between.

There was something about that particular view... Were Paul an artist or poet, he might have been better equipped to process, even express its evocative appeal. It beckoned to him, that much was clear. Following their day out, taking in sights and shops, Paul sat gazing out at the bay, its cold blue water nearly enclosed by thin arms of land, fenced in by the evergreens upon them. Gulls swooped, yellowing leaves teetered in the breeze and the crooked hump of Mt. Cadillac stood soft and blue beyond.

He watched the water and the sky, each darkening, subtly transforming as the sun set and wispy colors made insinuations softer than smears.

"I have to go down," Paul said.

"Supper's almost ready," Sandra called through steam, from inside the cabin proper.

"Just for a minute," Paul said.

Dusk was quickly becoming night outside the windows and the thick pines had merged darkly into the sky. Only the water showed, a bluish, moon-like pallor beyond the rustling brush.

"Paul, it's dark."

"I'll bring the flashlight. I'll be right back."

Sandra sighed. "All right…"

«« — »»

A single star had come out above the bay. Sandra saw it briefly through the trees as she went to fetch the spare flashlight from the car parked by the cabin. She could hear the lap and hiss of the water only minutes off, and shone her way behind the cabin where a worn path snaked through tall meadow growth, down to the pebbly dark and softly glinting water of the shore.

There were large rocks flung here and there, like unhewn furniture, and smooth stones of all sizes, tempting her to trip. There was mud and small cracking shells under her feet and, out in the black shifting water, projections of stone like beached and petrified whales, bearded with slippery seaweed.

"Paul?" She called into the dark.

Small waves whispered in.

"Paul?"

The battery light flashed around, illuminating stones like crouching bears, glaring on the water, casting tangled shadows in the exposed roots where tilted pines tottered on grassy eroded cliffs.

"Paul!"

There was only the bay stretching away into the distance, the empty rock-strewn beach, tidal pools cupped in cracked stone like skull sockets drowned in tears.

Running, tripping, running, Sandra made her way back to the cabin. She found her phone and called Linda and Dan, the proprietors. They came over from their small on site house and the three of them went down to the shore. There was still no sign of Paul.

Local police, search parties, even two Coast Guard boats could not locate Paul, dead or alive, near or in the water. A single star watched the commotion below and stared back up at itself from the cold dark water.

«« — »»

There was a thin footpath beaten through the meadow behind the cabins. Paul followed this through tall, dimming bushes, clusters of yarrow, pines too small to be Christmas trees, stalks of goldenrod and the dying white of Queen-Anne's-lace. The path forced him to duck through a low tunnel of pine boughs before delivering him to the shore. Thick roots, almost like steps, invited him down and out into the ocean air.

Paul and a single star spied each other. It was perched above the bay, high in the expansive sky. It made a soft echo in the water and from somewhere came the hollow call of a loon.

Gingerly, Paul moved closer to the surf, over the rough and smooth stones. The air was decidedly cooler now that the sun had gone down and it drifted in, an invisible tide above the water. Paul breathed it in, its thick salt, its chill, and he sighed. He took it all in with a good long look, then turned back toward the trail.

A flashlight led him through the murky meadow and he could see a light in the kitchen window of the cabin. The lobsters had to be about ready, he imagined. Three hollow steps up to the door and he was in. The door thumped shut behind him and he walked into the cabin and started to say something about the star.

"Sandra?"

The pot was rattling on the gas stove and steam was rushing out, rising from the gap beneath the lid. Sandra was not in the main chamber. The door to the cramped phone booth of a bathroom was open, but she was not there either.

"Sandra?"

He checked the car and around the cabin, went back to the shore. Only waves whispering in darkness.

A call to Linda and Dan would follow, and the police and the Coast Guard after that, but Sandra would not be found. There was nothing, Paul discovered, returning to cabin 13, but the big dented pot on the stove, the two lobsters inside, their great claws bound with wide rubber bands, kicking and scratching against the metal confines as they were steamed alive.

THIN
WALLS

don't mean to frighten you, but there's something strange about this place. A number of things actually. That smell has gotten worse for one and the plumbing makes terrible noises—mostly at night. The landlord keeps promising to look into it, but I keep wondering when. Maybe I'm just being neurotic, maybe half of these things are just my imagination.

It didn't seem like such a bad place two weeks ago when I moved in—a modest flat in a compartmentalized old Victorian on Baxter Street. It must have been impressive in its day. I imagine it was greying and abandoned before the landlord scoffed it up and sectioned it into rental units. Much of the old time charm is gone, hidden behind color-less latex paint and linoleum, the wide spaces made box-like by the addition of new walls. The modern building materials are cheap—the ancient horsehair plaster replaced by blue board—I could kick holes through the walls.

My sense of privacy is compromised here, because of these thin walls. I can hear the woman next door so distinctly…I imagine she can hear me just as well. Our bathrooms are like conjoined twins, separated by a thin membrane. Her tub seems to be parallel to mine, set only feet away, the plumbing consolidated within the flimsy wall. I'm afraid to urinate for fear that she's listening (I have a bashful bladder) and when I do, it sounds like I'm in an auditorium! I'll have to put a small radio in there and play it whenever I need to go.

The woman is not bad so far as neighbors go; no loud music, no blaring television. There was that time last week when she had a big fight with her boyfriend, but he hasn't been back. He slammed the door and I heard him pound down the stairs before he drove away. I haven't seen his car again, though looking down from my apartment, the parking area is poorly lit and the cars are dark huddled things.

I don't know the woman's name and we only spoke once, a simple hello while I was carrying my boxes in. I really ought to start unpacking. She's pretty in a somber kind of way with straight dark hair, dark eyes. She gave me the impression that she's shy. Who knows, maybe her boyfriend is out of the picture for good and now that I'm single again, well… No, I'm too damned shy for *that*, too fractured inside.

The days get dark so early now. I can't believe it's November already. I'll have to change the calendar. It's the only thing on the walls so far. I need to get more lights in this place, too—it's so gloomy. Even with every lamp (about the only things I've unpacked) going, I can't seem to chase off the shadows. These rooms are like boxes piled with my boxes.

Did I mention the plumbing? The toilet runs, the tub faucet drips, the pipes in the wall moan. The steam radiators hiss. It's like there are snakes in the walls, though I know that can't be true—there wouldn't be snakes in new walls.

It's pretty late and its quiet out on the street. I should really get to bed. My bladder is nagging me. Surely the girl next door is asleep by now. I haven't heard her all night. Funny, come to think of it, I haven't heard much from her in several days. I used to hear the dim clatter of her kitchen pans and her soft steps as she paced.

Okay, I'll be brave—the bladder wins again. The bathroom is small and dark, dominated by an old claw foot tub (one of the few charming things in the place). I stand over the toilet and start to relieve myself when I hear a soft noise from the wall. She's crying.

«« — »»

The holidays will be hard on me this year. I picture myself sitting in this dreary place eating a frozen turkey dinner from the microwave. How self-pitying! My sister will likely invite me over. Hell, I'll have to learn how to smile again. On second thought, maybe I'd be better off with the microwave feast. Don't know as I'm quite up for smiling yet.

I wonder if the woman next door has family. She must have friends or something because someone's been trying to call her. Maybe it's that bastard boyfriend who'd yelled at her, told her to go ahead and slit her wrists when he was leaving that time.

I unpacked a few books tonight. I noticed that Sarah had mutilated one, a collection of Thomas Hardy poems she'd given me when I turned thirty. She, at some point, close to the end one would hope, had cut off the top of the inner page where she had written a loving inscription. I wondered if the other books she had given me over the years had been similarly abridged and decided against unpacking anymore.

It's been damp and the November air seems to have put a grey chill in my bones. This is not the warmest place I've stayed in. Maybe a good hot soak will help. I run the tub until the steam erases my face from the mirror and I lower myself into the womb of water, rest my head on a rolled up towel. I close my eyes and try to think of nothing.

I can hear the soft whispering of the radiator, the heat just building into it, and the faucet going drip, drip, drip. Steam wisps off the water like a pond on an October morning. But there's November rain at the window and a sound from behind the thin wall. It's the dark-haired woman, awake at this late hour. She sounds so close—she too must be in the tub. I imagine her naked in the water, only feet away behind a wall I could put a fist through. Naked, smooth, stretched out in the water only feet, only inches away. She's weeping.

《《──》》

This is getting ridiculous! That smell can not be sanitary. Maybe the toilet drain in the wall is leaking or backed up or something. Surely the woman can smell it too. Maybe if several tenants complained, the apathetic landlord might take some action.

Thanksgiving is getting closer and today it looked like snow. I wonder what type of plowing the landlord will provide this winter. From my window, overlooking Baxter street, I can see the old New England houses darkening against a sombrous sky. No sky broods like a November sky.

My rooms still sit empty; I need to buy some furniture. My

neighbor's phone rings—she does not answer. The caller tries again without success. I have not seen her in the hall since that time when I was moving in. I imagine I'd be embarrassed if I did run into her, seeing as she's likely heard too much of my intimate little world.

I feel so sorry for her. She wept the whole time I was in the tub (my soak abbreviated for that very reason). That fellow must have broken her heart. Tonight I plan to stay up even later before getting into the tub; I'll wait her out. I'm a night owl, after all, and I shouldn't think that she'd be up to bathe at 4:00 am.

Midnight...quiet. One, two...not a sound from next door. Three...she must be sleeping; the only sound is the dripping of the faucet echoing in my tub...drip, drip, drip.

I seem to have underestimated her... As soon as I submerged myself in the steam and heat of the water, I heard her voice, soft at first, from behind the bland wall. I stretched out and closed my eyes, put a warm, damp face cloth over them. Damn! I can't relax with her sobbing like that. She's sobbing! Sobbing!

I picture her in her tub and it's strange—but this whole place is strange...the hissing, the dripping, the gurgling pipes and that stench. I picture her naked, lying slack in rust-colored water, staring at the wall, not blinking. I hear her sobbing, sobbing!

What is that horrible smell? I must call the landlord in the morning.

HALLOWEEN TEA

October looked good on the old town, Audrey thought, meandering in her car, reacquainting herself with the memories which were Eastborough. The town had grown considerably since she was young, but there remained an abundance of New England charm that developers had not managed to spoil. While there were several shopping centers on the outskirts and numerous business structures looming along Route 9, down in the old town proper autumn found a graceful haunt.

Audrey's first stop was the cemetery. Her long tan coat and auburn hair fluttered as she crunched up a hill overlooking adjacent farmland. There were more monuments than she recalled, the smallest of these half-submerged in fallen leaves beneath an ancient maple. She found the stone marked Emily and knelt.

Fingers reached to gently brush the cool marble and a tear fell to kiss the autumn's leafy cheek. She set a small pumpkin beside the stone and smiled sadly. "Happy Halloween," she whispered.

Audrey rose and a soft wind breathed, the pooled leaves trembling. The sun passed behind the western horizon, where naked trees reared in dark tangles against the sky's milky bronze.

《《——》》

"Hello?" It was an old woman's voice, a voice gone grey, straining as if muffled with webs.

"Hi, Mrs. Howe? This is Audrey Putnum."

There was a pause. "Audrey, good heavens, what a surprise, my dear!"

Audrey grinned. "It's so good to hear you. Guess what...I'm calling from the Eastborough Inn."

The old voice shed some of its webs. "You're in town! How nice! Why, I haven't seen you in so many years. Do you think you might find time to drop by?"

"Absolutely, with one minor condition. You remember what we used to do every Halloween?"

Mrs. Howe was hesitant. "Yes, we had a tea."

"Well, I just happen to have two fat pumpkins here, and I was thinking maybe we could..."

"Oh, Audrey, I'm so tired these days, I don't think I'm up to it. The place is such a mess and all. I haven't been well."

Audrey's voice returned, patiently bright. "I think a Halloween tea would do you good. I'll do all the work..."

Mrs. Howe agreed reluctantly and hung up the phone. She sat in the dimness of her living room, amidst the shadows that smelled like old newspapers. She gazed over at the framed picture of a little girl with smile-sparked eyes and hair of braided flax. The image was sun-faded, blurring to sepia, like a leaf turning.

Audrey had been Emily's best friend. For years, following the accident, Audrey had still come around. They had helped to heal one another, filling the chilled hollows of their hearts with warm cookies and jelly-souled tarts. There was iced tea in summer when the sweat ran like tears and laughter to fend off the winter's shrill dusk. They had shared long afternoons of talk and tea, carving their own brief traditions upon the rushing years, until even those gave way to the inevitability of distance. Audrey sought her dreams in a far-off state. Then there were only letters and cards, the occasional call.

Mrs. Howe brushed the warm trickle from her cheek and headed for the kitchen. For long hours of the night she bustled, dusting off her pans and cookie sheets, once more filling dark corners with the warm aroma of baking.

Then it was up into the creaky attic, wobbling amidst precarious heaps. A bare bulb rocked and treacle shadows poured as she sought out her old boxes of Halloween treasures. She smiled, unraveling them; ceramic figures lovingly packed in crinkly newspaper shrouds, candles and cut-outs like rediscovered friends. With so much to do, Mrs. Howe forgot how sickly she had been, how tired before Audrey's call. She spent much of the night whisking through the old house like an autumn breeze.

It was well after midnight when something started scratching at the back door. Mrs. Howe put down the small plastic witch she'd been holding and was moving toward the kitchen when she suffered one of her spells. Dizziness came over her, and there was the strange burning in her chest, as if some small internal blotch of darkness ached to spread, gnawing her away to nothing. A trembling hand reached the knob and pulled the door open.

A leafy sigh of wind gushed into the kitchen as Mrs. Howe looked down at the doorstep. The breeze cooled the burning in her chest, and she smiled like a jack-o'-lantern at the sight of a fat black cat sitting there, grinning up at her.

《《—》》

There was something in the air. It was more subtle than when Audrey had been younger, but it was still there, flitting leaf-like, fluttering bat-like through the rooms of her heart on a moon-frosted breeze. It was an anticipatory sensation that drew her like some ancient gravity. It beckoned to her with rattling cornstalk voices, singing cider-perfume through leaf-sparse branches. Only one day a year she felt it, on the afternoon of October 31st, when all the world seemed to tilt toward the mystical night.

Familiar streets passed through the woman's windshield. Most of the urgent colors had passed; still there were sporadic gushes of crimson and amber. The houses were old, high things, some still enveloped in mantles of maple cadmium.

Audrey could remember braving those stairs, standing in puddles of porch light as screen doors whined and towering adults chuckled down. Treats had rained into her hungry chocolate-breathed bag. How the houses had loomed then, the streets stretching off—elastic charcoal murals—jack-o'-lanterns dappling; the smell of wood smoke ethereal and enticing.

««—»»

Coppery rays of afternoon sunlight were slanting through the trees when Audrey pulled up outside Mrs. Howe's house. The place looked tired, overgrown and weedy, but there was a thrill of familiarity. A ghost of coziness. Audrey carried a shopping bag full of goodies onto the porch, then went back to get the pumpkins.

She knocked. The door opened.

"Trick or treat!" Audrey exclaimed.

They hugged. Mrs. Howe looked over the younger woman, who was in her mid-thirties; pretty, with chocolate eyes and auburn hair. She wore a black skirt and a peach-colored sweater. Little gold skull earrings gleamed.

Mrs. Howe was willowy, grey, her eyes the blue of a September sky, still glinting from out of the bark-like creases of her flesh. She wore a long black gown and shawl.

"Come in, come in!"

Candles lit the foyer, like some initiatory tunnel leading into the heart of the season. Indeed, the place was something of a Halloween decoration museum, or shrine. Mrs. Howe's extensive collection included rare and antiquated treasures, from old faded Dennison cutouts to imported German papier-mache vegetable spirits dating from 1900. A slender glass black cat, obviously a deco-inspired work, seemed ready to pounce from the bookcase as they entered the living room.

Audrey ducked beneath a brittle construction-paper chain she and Emily had made in fourth grade. The orange had faded to a dusty peach and the black had gone grey.

A ponderous cat waddled out of the shadows, rubbing against Audrey's ankles.

"Basil!" She reached down to stroke the warm purring blackness.

They walked deeper into the living room, where a tape of low-rumbling organ music was playing. Audrey smiled, delighted. A ceramic skull sat on the table in a nest of colorful leaves, surrounded by plates loaded with pastries, cheeses, apples and nuts. She wagged her head. "I thought you were too tired…"

"So did I," Mrs. Howe admitted.

"It's lovely." Audrey glanced over at a picture of Emily dressed as a bunny, the picture frame carefully ringed in bittersweet. Something caught in her throat.

"So," Mrs. Howe said, clapping her hands together, "where are those pumpkins?"

«« — »»

They stood on the porch, admiring their handiwork, as purple saturated the dusk sky. The carved pumpkins flanked the door, bright tongues flicking behind lipless mouths, the freshly cut features beading with moisture.

Audrey turned, looking up and down the street. They were already out—small figures rustling along shaded sidewalks, ectoplasmic sheets swaying, miniature witches giggling and shrieking. The October sun seemed to crackle as it died behind the skeleton trees.

"I was reading about the history of Halloween," Mrs. Howe said, leaning on the porch railing, eyeing the last brassy glimmers. "This night was New Year's Eve to the ancient Celts. They thought the old year died at sunset and the new year didn't start until sunrise on November 1st. The period between was a timeless place when the dead returned…"

Audrey smiled, inhaling the leaves and wood smoke and candle-warmed pumpkins. She nodded.

Mrs. Howe slumped forward, catching a porch beam for support. She put a hand to her chest and grimaced.

"Mrs. Howe!"

"I'm all right…just a little dizzy."

Audrey looked concerned, taking a step closer, taking the woman's frail arm.

"Shall we have tea, Audrey?"

"Yes."

«« — »»

Earl Grey with orange food-coloring. Old radio shows on the tape player—Arch Obler's *Lights Out!*. Orson Welles' *War of the Worlds*. Trick-or-treaters kicked through jaundice leaves and knocked and chanted at the gourd-guarded door. A lidded stew pot sat on a stove burner, the popcorn kernels inside kicking like rain on tin. Had there ever been such a magic night?

The hours crept by. They sat by the fireplace as birch crackled in its flickering bed of flame, painting their shadows as long ghastly things. Mulled cider followed the tea and Mrs. Howe read M.R. James' *Oh Whistle and I'll Come to You, My Lad* with Basil curled humming in her lap.

The candy-hunters had retired to their own cozy abodes and even the older pranksters had turned the streets over to the scurrying patrols of citrine leaves. The hours ticked as they reminisced, one, two, three in the morning.

The pumpkins burned out and a gentle drizzle fell. Audrey grew drowsy, slumped in her wing chair. The fireplace pulsed with coals, casting a serene glow on the picture of little Emily.

«« — »»

The knock woke Audrey.

"Oh, I must have dozed off."

Mrs. Howe sat forward. "I'll get it."

Basil leapt down from the old woman's lap and climbed up onto Audrey. He purred as he always had, those many years ago, rubbing his head against the woman's chin. He had that "old cozy" smell that the house did.

Mrs. Howe made for the front door, shuffling along in her black gown. Audrey glanced at the clock. There were only minutes left until dawn. She leaned forward so that she could see out into the foyer.

The door opened, welcoming in the last of October's cool exhalations. A small child stood on the porch. She was so unnaturally thin that her faded bunny suit hung on her frame like the skin of a hound. Flaxen braids framed the mask and she looked up at the old woman through its hollow eyes. The girl held out a pale hand and Mrs. Howe took it, stepping outside with her, out into the leaves and fading darkness.

Basil perked, turning toward the breeze. It occurred to Audrey, at last, as she sat stroking his dark fur, that Basil had died in his sleep many years before. The cat gave a meow and leapt down, pattering across the room, through the hallway and out behind Mrs. Howe and the little girl.

The door swung shut. Audrey sat by the fireplace, a smile on her lips as the first flush of dawn illuminated the lacy frost on the living room windows.

"Happy Halloween," she whispered.

THE
GIRL
IN THE
ATTIC

"**Y**ou're okay. You're fine."

Ron took a deep breath and surveyed himself in the mirror. A facade of composure stared back through a dull constellation of toothpaste spatters.

"You can do it, Ron," he told himself, though the voice sounded brittle with tension.

"Damn it!"

He yanked a face cloth from a towel rack, turned the faucet on so it poured out angrily, dunked the cloth in and scrubbed maniacally at the mirror. His features seemed to clench in towards each other with the gravity of neurotic intensity. The spatters smeared first, then were gone.

It was as if an irritating itch had been subdued. Ron neatly folded the wash cloth and placed it in its proper place. He stood observing himself again; once more the glass contained a clean-shaven, trim-haired, even-tempered image of control.

"There," Ron said.

He lived in an attic apartment. Immaculate. An air conditioner hummed. Spread across a desk in one corner of the living room was an orderly buffet of note papers and books. Ron leaned into his reading, digesting each line.

There were images to take in as well. Human shapes like maps of red and blue highways. The complex and scraggly lines that comprised the nervous system. Photographs of plump, loosely shaped organs. The things a medical student was required to look upon.

The freak genius of nature had disclosed its maddening love of detail when it assembled the human machine. Ron had seen under the hood of that vehicle, looked at the tubes and wires, seen the mushy grey computer slipped from its bone container. For all the intricacies of it, he could not understand how the damn thing worked. All the parts were there—but what sparked them to life? Muscle, blood and neurons needed something to set them in motion. What? The dissections he had witnessed always left that question hanging heavy in his mind.

The phone rang. Shrill distraction. Ron sighed and waited for his answering machine to come on.

"Hello. I can't come to the phone right now…"

After the beep, the caller's voice stumbled. "Ronny? Hey, man, are you there?"

Ron's guts tensed. Memories like a sour taste came seeping.

"Ronny, pick up, kid, please!"

Ron mumbled to himself, "Not this, not now…"

The voice was emphatic, edged with desperation. "Ronny, it's important; I need your help. Please. I know you're there!"

Manipulating bastard, Ron thought. He snatched the receiver.

"What trouble are you in now, Jimmy?"

Ronny had been through this before, getting late night calls from the older brother whose life was without control or direction. Jimmy was selfish, self-destructive, a scavenger preying on good-hearted fools like himself.

"Oh, thank God, you had me worried." Nervous little laugh. "You're there."

"Yeah," Ron felt guilty for sounding so impatient. "So what is it? You need bail money? Cindy threw you out again?"

"No, man, no…it's…it's really fucked up."

"Well, what is it?"

"It's crazy."

"I bet it's crazy. You want to know what's crazy? Calling me at quarter after midnight when I'm cramming for a big exam is crazy."

Jimmy's voice sounded less party-ravaged; it softened now, as if he were shrinking away from the phone. "Forget it, kid, I'm sorry. You got your shit together now, you don't need my problems, right? I should leave you alone, Christ, I shouldn't be such a freaking pest. I'll go. Never mind."

Long silence.

"Where are you?" Ron asked.

"Mike Wilson's house. I've been stayin' here for two months. Cindy dumped me."

Ronny sighed. "So what do you want, Jimmy?"

Ron felt queasy as he listened to the fear that swelled in his brother's drunken words. "I'm in big trouble. Me and Mike picked up this chick, and...oh, shit, just please come out. I gotta go."

Ron could hear a commotion in the background, a man's voice yelling, things slamming.

"Jimmy, you there?"

"Yeah, yeah. Hey, you still got my gun?"

Pause. "Yes..."

"Bring it, okay?"

"Give me a break! What do you need a gun for?"

Click.

Ron tried calling back several times, but received no answer.

«« — »»

It was a twenty-minute drive to Upton. The humid air sponged pungent secrets from the dense vegetation lining the road. The layered odors swept Ron's face as the wind poured through his windows. There was an almost sex-like quality to it—thick, moist, too heavy to be likened to perfume. It was as if he were inhaling the chirping night-green of nature's crotch.

"I must be nuts," Ron observed.

He was trembling. What hellish mess was he getting himself into?

"I shouldn't have brought the gun. I shouldn't have." The pistol had belonged to Jimmy, who had to give up his license after firing the .357 magnum into the air at a Fourth of July party. Ron had mercifully bought it for target shooting.

What had Jimmy said? Something about a girl. Had Jimmy hit on some dangerous drug dealer's girlfriend? Had he picked up a girl who

then proceeded to OD? Had he raped somebody? Was he now conse-
quently hiding from police or a shotgun-toting father?

"It's not fair. I'm doing something with my life, I'm going to be a
doctor. I don't throw my life away partying anymore. I've risen above
that. I've got things under control. I don't need this bullshit!"

A few more rambling side streets and he'd be there. The edge of
town—mostly woods and pasture, with the occasional unkempt old
New England farmhouse. No other traffic. Tension playing cat's-cradle
with his intestines.

A clutter of overgrown shrubs marked the long dirt driveway. The
tall building stood half buried in trees, its Colonial elegance long since
lost to years of neglect and raucous parties. Headlights swept across
chipping paint as Ron pulled up and parked.

He sat there, listening. Watching. Thick encircling blackness of
summer-heavy trees. Shrill crickets, coy fireflies. A primer-scorched
Buick parked nearby. He looked at the house's windows, some with
light showing through the screens, the bathroom where a beach towel
served as a curtain, displaying an upside-down Snoopy. No signs of
movement in there.

He was tempted to leave, but he couldn't. Though Jimmy was a jerk
who would use and exploit any willing victim, Ron loved his brother.
He did decide to leave the gun in the car, though.

Ron shut his car door as quietly as possible and moved up the stone
steps to the porch. Audible ache from sagging boards beneath his
stealthy sneakers. Moths like fluttery lichen at the screen door.

"Hello?" Ron called.

It was a mess inside, from what he could see. He hated clutter.

"Hello?" Louder.

A figure lurched into view, arms flung out, the palms slapping the
door frame, the face coming close to the screen with bulging eyes,
exhaling a gust of alcohol-tainted breath. Jimmy's face was a swarm
with beads of sweat, the eyes reaching out from the stubble and wetness.

"Ronny, thank God, man, you made it!"

Ron stepped back, blinking. "What are you on? You look like hell."

"I'm on fuckin' adrenaline, man," Jimmy said, shaking his head.

"That's not what your breath smells like."

Jimmy squealed the screen door open, grabbed Ron's arm and
dragged him inside. The house branched out from this cramped hall

area. The air reeked; cigarette smoke from the living room, garbage from the kitchen. It was hot.

"This had better be important, Jimmy, and I'll tell you right now, I'm not lending you any money."

Jimmy's face was puffy and coarse compared with Ron's shaven and scrubbed youthfulness. His eyes toted bags. His hair was darker, longer, disarrayed.

"I don't need cash, kid…I don't know what I need. I don't know what to do, you're the only person I could think to call."

If Ron didn't know better he'd have thought Jimmy was about to cry.

"What is it, Jim?"

Jimmy gulped, wiped a hand across his face and leaned closer. Ron felt uneasy in the confines, trapped by the stale hot air, the stench of rotting food from the kitchen, Jimmy's sweaty odor and beer-exhalations.

The older brother's eyes rolled about, big and fear-crazed as he related his story. "Me and Mike went to a party tonight out in Blackstone. We were comin' back when we saw this girl walking on the side of the road, way out in the sticks, ya know? So we ask, we asked her if she wanted a ride. She said yeah, sure. So we ended up at the sand pits with her, gettin' high."

Ron was nodding, eager to have this over with, to be home in his clean orderly world, safe in bed with the air conditioner humming him to sleep.

"This chick was really nice—I think she said she was from Northbridge. Anyway, she's actin' pretty horny, so we start pawin' at her and pretty soon we're doin' her on a blanket, right there in the sand pits."

"Great," Ron said, sarcasm venting tension, "I'm happy for you."

Jimmy's eyes bobbed from side to side. "She flipped out. Right as I'm banging her she starts goin', 'Kill me! Kill me! Please kill me!' I didn't know what to think. I was pretty wrecked, ya know. So I kind of choked her some, and she started getting into it big time, goin' like mad. So I kept choking her and she was still telling me to kill her, and then she passed out."

Jimmy paused, stared at the moths clicking against the screen trying to gain entry, wiped his face with a trembling hand.

OVER THE DARKENING FIELDS

OVER THE DARKENING FIELDS

"I didn't think, I thought she was just knocked out, but she was dead."

Ron exploded. "You loser! You moron! Some drugged-out weirdo girl tells you to kill her so you kill her? Jesus! My God, you murdered somebody!"

"Sshhhh! Wait, wait, that's not all of it. Hold on, Ronny. Listen—we got scared and took off -"

"You left her there?"

"Yeah. We dumped her behind some bushes. So we took off and came home here. Well, the lights were on when we pulled in. I saw a girl walk by in the window...I figured Cindy had come by looking for me. So we go in and there's this fuckin' dead chick! She's up and walking around, but she's dead!"

"You thought she was dead, but she was obviously just unconscious."

"No, no—she's dead."

"You're drunk, her pulse was low, you missed it when you checked."

"No. No way."

"Then where's the body?"

"Walking around in the attic. Mike went up there when we were on the phone. He didn't come down."

Ron grinned nervously. "This is a joke, right?"

Jimmy shook his head. His eyes pleaded.

"You've done too many drugs, then. Okay, so you believe it—well, I don't. What did you want a gun for, to kill a dead girl?"

"Did you bring it?"

"No. I forgot. So show me this zombie of yours, because I have to get up early tomorrow and take a test. Let's have a look."

"Not me, I ain't going up there."

"Look, what did you bring me here for? I'm tired, I'm nervous. Either we go up or I'm out of here."

"Okay, okay..."

《《——》》

They passed through the living room where Salvation Army furniture hosted a television and stereo and beer cans served as knickknacks.

Stairs led to the second floor where a sharp turn brought them to another, more narrow set of stairs.

Jimmy hung back. "She's up there."

Ron looked up at a once-white door. Thick lead paint. A bare bulb poking out from a socket to one side, activated by a switch at the bottom. The brothers turned to look at each other when they heard someone pad across the floor overhead.

"See…" Jimmy whispered.

Ron shuddered. "You said Mike's up there?"

"Yeah."

"They're probably screwing."

"She's dead!"

"That wouldn't stop Mike," Ron joked bitterly.

Ron felt uneasy about this, but he knew that whatever was up there was not a dead thing. He started up, half wishing that he had brought the gun. Jimmy stayed a few steps below, fear-pumped eyes leading him.

Fingers lingered in the air over the doorknob. It was suffocating in the stairwell. On the other side of the door, something fell and rolled, a bottle perhaps. Ron touched the knob, twisted.

A dark tunnel opened up as the door swung in. A window on either side bled pale blue night from the outside. Clutter. Old furniture created a maze of shadowy obstacles. Other chambers opened off this main one. There could have been twenty dead girls in there, for all Ron knew.

"Hello?" Ron's voice sounded.

Jimmy cringed. "Don't call it, man," he whispered.

Ron turned around. "The lights…"

"There aren't any."

"Great."

Movement off to the right. Ron squinted. An old bedroom bureau with a mounted mirror on top showed his reflection through dust and webs. Though Jimmy was armed with a large kitchen knife, he let his unarmed brother lead the way.

The air up here on the third floor was far worse than on the other two levels. There was no ventilation. Something smelled, possibly the garbage in the kitchen trailing up.

Ron's hand brushed an old chair, webs, both sticky and dry, pasting themselves to his flesh. He rubbed at the irritating substance and proceeded slowly. They were halfway through the first room, close to the other door openings.

"There!" Jimmy hissed.

A figure pulled back shyly from the doorway on the right. Ron caught a glimpse of long light hair. He stepped quicker, his heart betraying the reasoning of his mind. The girl was probably just whacked out on something…

He rounded the big old bureau and peered into the other room. There was more light in there, and, of course, more clutter. There were boards, ancient shingles, even a saggy mattress propped against one wall. The girl stood in the center of the room.

"Hello…" Ron ventured.

She was naked, pale, her face vague, the features only blurred shadows, the body mostly masked in the darkness. She stepped back slowly and moved behind a curtain of plywood. Only the face, with long hair trailing, poked out—mournful sockets of shadow for eyes.

"Hi. Um, are you okay? I'm a medical student. We won't hurt you."

Ron heard bare feet fidgeting on ancient floorboards, and a soft hiss of a voice, a single, almost imperceptible word: "Dead."

Jimmy hovered in the doorway while Ron carried himself closer. His foot hit something solid. He knelt, felt cloth, buttons, wetness. Fingers climbed up to a face. He felt the surface of staring eyes, room temperature flesh.

"Oh my God—it's Mike!"

Her scream resounded deafeningly in the cramped attic room. The girl threw herself upon Ron and caught his shoulder in her teeth, knocking him to the floor, straddling him.

"Ahhhh! Get her off! Hey!"

The girl's hand slipped over Ron's mouth and shoved his head back hard against the floor. He saw her grey breasts jiggling above him, her shadowy stare and grimace. She had his hair now, hammering away with his skull until the world flitted in and out of darkness.

Great flowers of light faded in Ron's head, lucidity returning, the sound of scuffling close. Two blurry figures danced above him, dark limbs flailing the dense air, the girl's haze-colored hair like a ghostly flag.

Ron struggled to his feet as the wrestling pair went toppling into attic debris; leaning boards clattered down, a lampshade crumpled, a rusty tin of roofing nails scattered. Ron saw the kitchen knife on the floor where Jimmy must have dropped it. He grabbed the handle and rushed forward to save his brother.

The girl had her thumbs in Jimmy's mouth, stretching his cheeks back at painful angles, thrashing her head from side to side so that her hair lapped about her bare shoulders. Ron pounded the knife into her back—she turned, grimacing. Jimmy scrabbled free and grabbed Ron by the arm, pulling him toward one of the other rooms.

The girl thumped after them; Ron felt her fingers at his back, like icy twigs snaring in his shirt. They slammed the door shut behind them, bracing it with their weight as her weight banged against it.

Ron turned to his brother. "She is dead…"

Jimmy stared back and nodded. "I told you."

The girl drummed on the door, the vibrations loosing bits of peeling paint which dropped to the floor like petrified moths. There was a single window at the far end of this little room, but the brothers dared not leave the door untended, besides, they were three floors up and even if they could call out for help, there were no neighbors close enough to hear. So they stood there for hours, pressed against the old white wood as dead fists pounded and pounded and pounded.

The lone window gradually lightened, birds stirred noisily, dusty beams crept into the hot attic room and the thumping at the door waned, like a slowing heart, ceasing altogether when the sun hefted itself up over the horizon of dense trees. The brothers heard something thud heavily on the floor beyond the door.

They waited several long minutes before opening the door. She was face down, the knife still deep in her naked back, which had bled very little, considering the intrusion of metal. The dead girl at last seemed dead.

《《—》》

Mike and the girl were cocooned in old sheets, carried out to Ron's car and crammed into the trunk. The brothers tossed a shovel into the back seat and then climbed into the front where the magnum revolver sat between them. Ron started the engine and spun the wheel, carving half moons into the dirt drive. They headed for the sand pits where the nightmare had begun; it was, after all, a good place to hide bodies.

"This is crazy," Ron muttered, trembling.

"You want to try explaining this to the cops?" Jimmy snorted. "Hey—careful!"

Tires shrieked, the car veered along a winding back road. Ron was too shaken, too drained to be driving, but he was not about to let Jimmy behind the wheel; his breath was still heavy with alcohol.

"Slow down, Ronny, or we'll all be dead!"

Ron didn't see the police car—nestled back in some bushes at the mouth of a dirt road—until it was too late. "Shit!"

The police car pulled out and followed them. Blue lights flashed.

Ron flicked his eyes to the speedometer; the car was traveling near sixty miles an hour in a thirty-mile zone. "Shit, shit, shit! Hide the gun, Jimmy!"

The car eased to the side of the road; the cruiser floated up close in the rearview mirror. A man stepped out and approached, a hand at his hip. Dark glasses stared in at the two jittery men who stared back with too-wide eyes.

"You gentlemen in a hurry or what?" the officer asked.

Ron, still clutching the wheel, shook his head. "No."

"License and registration, please…"

Ron reached instinctively for the glove compartment where he kept the car's registration along with the manual and neatly folded maps. The door dropped open and the magnum slid out; Jimmy instinctively reached to catch it, moving too quickly, grabbing the handle. There was a blur to Ron's left as the policeman drew his automatic and fired once into the car. The loud popping reverberated through the vehicle as Jimmy slumped back in his seat; his head dropped forward, chin resting on the wet red of his chest.

《《——》》

The jury sentenced Ron to two consecutive life terms for the murders of Mike and the girl (who remained a Jane Doe), and while he had attempted to convince them that he had tried to stop his brother Jimmy from killing them, the evidence against him was too strong. His bloody fingerprints were found on Mike's face and shirt and his fingerprints were also discovered on the handle of the kitchen knife still protruding from the dead girl's back when she was taken from the trunk of his car. The shovel in the back seat did not help matters.

Ron kept his cell immaculately clean, even the newspaper clippings he had collected were stored in a tidy pile in a manila envelope. The articles spanned several months, each concerning vandalism at the grave of the dead girl, whose identity remained unknown. She had been buried in a section of cemetery where the destitute were interred, with nothing more than a small numbered disc of cement to remind the world that she had existed. Several times the burial site had been disturbed in the middle of the night, perhaps by prank-minded teenagers, drawn to that particular grave due to the grisly and publicized nature of the girl's death.

According to a report in the morning paper, the vandals had outdone themselves at last; not only had they mussed the earth where the girl lay; they actually tunneled down to the coffin, opened it up and stole the body.

MILTON CRANE'S COLLECTION

The wind in the September trees had a somewhat plaintive sound, which had not been there all summer. William noticed it while in the upstairs bedroom, dressing for the day's solemn task. There was a restless maple outside the window to his right and thick pines with conducting limbs in the one opposite. The air was bright and cool, cheery, in contrast to what lay ahead.

In the kitchen, Karen was pacing with a phone in one hand and a coffee in the other. Her eyes were red and damp. She mouthed the name of her sister and William nodded. The sister, Judith, lived in East Sullivan, Maine; it would take her roughly six hours to drive down. Karen and Judith each represented the other's only living sibling, now that Milton was gone.

«« — »»

The foliage was only a hint of things to come, there in central Massachusetts, but here and there, along the drive from Hopkinton to Eastborough, there were emerging gems. The first leaves were on the lawns, and cartwheeling in the gutter when the car whisked past.

There were shady old streets and stately old houses—imposing Victorians, prim Colonials, salt boxes, capes. A long dirt drive through a tunnel of shade brought them face-to-face with Milton Crane's house.

It was an oddity of sorts, a modified Victorian of steep grey, the roofline high and sharp, projecting out over dull windows. An adjacent crumbling carriage house was folding in like ribs to feed gravity. While the neglected condition of the behemoth was itself rather startling, it was the odd tower-like structure rearing up from the high point of the conventional roof that commanded the eye.

The tower was round, part widow's watch, part church steeple, open at the top like a gazebo under a conical roof of grey shingles. William thought that it looked like a rotting wooden rocket. Milton had called it his "wind room."

The porch creaked and leaves ran scratching over the boards. Karen had the key and unlocked the door, which whined like a haunted thing when opened. It was grey inside, the lower rooms crowded with stacks of old newspapers. The retired history professor had saved papers dating back to the forties, even had some brittle specimens from the 1800s. The past was not something he chose to discard.

Even the kitchen was full of papers, and boxes of books covered the table and chairs. There were webs in the corners and in wispy arrangements about the clutter. The webs were abandoned—it looked as if they had netted little more than dust and grey light.

There was no television in the sitting room, only an old cathedral radio and a comfortably worn chair by a reading table. Karen reached down to touch the cushion where her brother had spent so many of his lonely hours. Her hand trembled.

The woman took in the room and smiled sadly. "He was a compulsive collector."

William nodded. "He was an interesting guy, Karen."

"Eccentric, you mean."

"Well, yeah, but in a good way."

Karen sniffled. "Yes, in a good way. He never hurt a fly."

"Although," William said, grinning mischievously, "he did have some trouble with the police a few times for standing naked in the tower."

Karen swatted at him halfheartedly. "Oh, stop it!"

William chuckled, "I'm not making it up."

Karen gazed up at the crumbling plaster of the ceiling. "You want to go upstairs?"

"Sure. What's up there, more papers?"

"I don't know; I haven't been up there since I was a kid. I really should have visited him more, but he didn't really like visitors."

«« —»»

Bundles of newspapers made the climb up the stairs somewhat treacherous. Karen saw finger trails through the dust on the banister, likely Milt's.

William stepped slowly behind his wife, ready to catch her if she fell. "Karen, do you remember that time he said he'd traveled back to the Kennedy assassination to get the scoop—"

Karen finished the thought. "But he wouldn't tell us who did it. He visited Lincoln's assassination too, and the wreck of the Hindenburg."

William said, "Gee, sounds kind of morbid."

"Oh no, it was all important history, that's what mattered. He claimed he was at the signing of the Declaration of Independence and the birth of Thomas Jefferson."

"Let's not forget the Salem witch trials and the shot heard round the world."

Milton's bedroom was the first of several on the second floor. It seemed smaller for all the boxes. There were no newspapers, but there were other odd collectibles. A civil war rifle in seemingly new condition, a circular soap dish (supposedly from the Titanic) with the White Star Line logo printed in red, also in mint condition. There was a pristine World War 1 gas mask and a small cardboard box containing a lock of hair and a small piece of paper that said: Washington.

Mulling over a dueling pistol, William looked up and noted, "Damn, these are better than any replicas I've ever seen."

Karen was hugging herself, staring at the bed. "Maybe they aren't."

"They wouldn't be in such good condition if they were actual period pieces. You don't suppose he could've afforded to have them custom crafted by somebody?"

Karen seemed not to hear; she sat on the edge of the bed and gazed at the pillow, rumpled, indented. She said, "Do people really die in their sleep? I mean, without waking up?"

"That's what they say."

"I hope its true," Karen said.

William picked up a framed photograph that showed the stout, pleasant faced Milton Crane standing with his arms around the shoulders of the Wright Brothers. "Pretty convincing fake," he muttered.

«« —»»

"Where's the Minotaur?" William asked upon entering the maze-like clutter of the attic.

Karen was downstairs going through Milt's closet looking for an appropriate suit to bury him in. She did not want to accompany her husband to the tower, didn't think it looked safe. Obviously she lacked her brother's sense of adventure.

Weaving his way through moth-ravaged furniture, more stacks of newspapers, more boxes, William found the bottom of a spiral metal staircase. Up into the clanging tube he went, slivers of light showing where the boards were failing. He could hear the muffled voice of a pigeon in the darkness above.

There was a hinged wooden hatch and then the dizzying openness and the crisp of September wind. The sky was clear blue and he could see the town—its roofs and trees. "The wind room," William said to the pigeon perched on the rail.

It would have been more dramatic, more mysterious if the crazy old fellow had been found dead up there, the launching place where he would apply his secret methods, capturing the wind, to speed him on his supposed journeys. Better yet—if the man had simply vanished, leaving only a cryptic note nailed to a beam there in the creaky tower. But Milton went in his sleep, earthbound and mortal and old. There was no mystery but for the one that causes obsession and compulsion to rear so boldly in certain individuals.

The wind was plaintive, high in the tower and the pigeon fluttered up and away.

«« —»»

Karen was still busy with her task, so William, having returned from the rickety wind room, decided to investigate the remaining bed-chambers.

"Damn," he muttered.

It was the strangest thing yet. Room after room lined with shelves full of empty glass jars of varying shape and size. Empty applesauce jars, pickle jars, mason jars, marshmallow fluff jars, jelly jars. All empty...thousands of them, row after row.

"Poor bastard," William said, "he was nuts."

In one room, he plucked a medium-sized jar from the shadows and webs and held it to the afternoon light. Definitely empty. He unscrewed the lid.

A chill burst of wind whistled up from the jar into William's face. He gasped and stepped back, dropping the jar, which shattered as it hit the floor. The wind hissed, dissipated, faded into the dusty air.

«« — »»

Karen looked pleased with herself. She had laid a suit out on the small bed and, having made her decision, was putting others back in the closet. She looked up to see William standing in the doorway with a bewildered smile on his face.

"William? *What is it?*"

Maybe he shouldn't tell her what he saw, he thought. But maybe he would...he had to tell someone.

THE DOLL

A young couple bought an old house. Moldy Victorian gingerbread. There were November sepia woods about and networks of forgotten dirt paths. Distant hills like solidified waves of fog.

The couple cleaned and painted, filled quiet rooms with saw shrieks and hammer blows. Slowly, rooms so dark for so long, became bright.

Between long hours of repair and restoration, the couple took chilly walks on tangled trails. One afternoon, with clouds like bruises dragging across the sky, they ventured into a little cemetery.

It was neglected and quaint. Epitaphs peeked through dried grass, speaking both poetic and pious. It was calm, near meditative, ancient.

Until the wife called out, "Come look at this."

At first she had mistaken the doll for a real little girl. Antique, she was laying face down on the grave of a child who had died at the age of seven. Its arms, outstretched in front, were stuck into the soil. The wife pulled it loose.

Porcelain head, clotted hair, faded dress. The smell of a musty attic. One eye was a hole; cracks formed lightning-jagged tear tracks. Muddy little lips.

《《——》》

Within a few days the snow began. The world received a gentle cleansing. A fireplace tossed orange highlights on the doll's chipped cheeks. She was propped up on a rocking chair in the living room. She watched the couple as they drank hot chocolate.

Into the night the snow accumulated, a wind moaning melancholy as flakes blew down like ghost locusts. Through drawn shades it glowed bluish. The couple slept, tucked in a familiar bed, in a now familiar room. Peaceful snug hours passed, and at night's deepest, coldest point...

Glass breaking! A sudden harsh sound. Surely one of the old tree branches out front, weighted with snow, had snapped, hitting a window.

The couple tossed on their robes and thumped downstairs. Into the living room, flicked on a light.

The heavy door was ajar. The storm door's window was shattered from slamming shut. Jagged pieces lay on the damp carpet.

The couple stared out through the remains of the fanged window at a trail of tiny footprints that headed off toward the old cemetery.

WINTER CENSUS

This isn't a story about the conventional horrors of homeless life; not that I couldn't fill volumes with that stuff. But since you ask me for the most disturbing thing I've seen...I'll tell you.

It was late December and I was a volunteer with a group working for the mayor's office. It was an annual event. Our task was to go around the city and take a count of all the homeless people we could find. It was only my second time, though I'd been involved with the shelters for several years, and I'd organized food drives and things of that nature going back nine or ten.

I was accompanied by a young guy named Don, who was an EMT, and Father Ed Willard, a priest who had dedicated so much time and soul to looking after the disadvantaged that he had been written up in a national news magazine and had made a number of appearances on local television. We were quite the dedicated crew.

The winter had been mild up until that night, generally speaking, though it's true what they say about New England weather—it can change in a flash. It's best not to get complacent, even with a long stretch of merciful temperatures. It can drop down to a windchill of thirty degrees below faster than you can say hypothermia.

That night we got the first real wintry stuff of the season. It was bitter cold and snowing pretty good. Windy too. A ragtag army of vehicles spread out to explore the city, armed with flashlights and blankets.

I don't mind telling you that the census adventure could be frightening at times. We would venture into some pretty rough areas and there were some scary characters around. Ever drive through Roxbury after dark? I think if I were to go again I'd want to carry a gun, especially after that night.

It didn't take us long. They were huddled in doorways, in alleys, in places you wouldn't believe. People can get pretty creative and fit their bodies into some strange places in order to get out of the cold.

We had to joke to keep each other's spirits up because the tragedy factor was so profound. I remember an old lady we found curled up on a grid to catch the heat that came up. She had a flattened refrigerator box over her head and snow had coated it. She was clinging to an old beat-up stuffed dog toy and her coat pockets were filled with empty bottles. She seemed to be somewhat retarded.

Images like this made me feel like murdering career welfare abusers. My tax dollars were doing nothing for that suffering old woman, while I'd known young "breed for bucks" mothers and smug young men who bragged about what a great country America was because (besides working a job) they benefited from food stamps and Medicare. One encounters a lot of injustice out in the streets.

Don thought the woman's breathing was bad and that she was a good candidate for frostbite. We decided to call an ambulance. Turns out she ended up losing a few toes.

Well, I'll get to the point, seeing as it's getting kind of late. We had gone into the north end, where there were a good deal of old brick buildings. We parked, then crunched along on the snow while flakes whirled down through the pink haze of the street lamps. Father Willard became concerned when he couldn't find a Viet Nam vet named Reggie who usually stayed in this particular indented area behind a building, between two dumpsters.

"Hey," Don had said, "look at this."

Don was pointing at what appeared to be drag marks, wide, as if someone had been pulled along the pavement on his back. We followed them out to the street and saw that they led to an alley, which, due to the snow, was not as dark as it normally would've been.

Don thought he saw someone extremely tall flit by the opening of the alley, but Father Willard said that Reggie was a very short man.

We were starting over, squinting through the slanting snowfall, when we saw these three strobe-like flashes of red come from inside that alley. We ran—I was the first one to see it.

At the far end of the alley, where the strewn trash was smoothed over in gentle waves by the accumulated white, there was a blackened heap of steaming human bones. The stench was enough to make you sick.

"Dear God," Father Willard said.

"What the hell happened?" I asked, squinting down at the pieces that were stacked like so much kindling.

"He must've built a fire to keep warm," Don offered weakly.

I wondered how he could have burned down so thoroughly—I mean, there was no sign of scorched clothing, no suggestion of skin, muscle or organs. There were only bones.

"Maybe," Don conjectured, "somebody killed him and set the corpse on fire."

I nodded. In these days when teenage kids were killing each other over sneakers and jackets, it was quite likely that someone would kill a poor homeless guy for kicks and then set him on fire. Hopefully he was already dead before the flames were lit. Although this theory offered a reasonable explanation as to how the man was burned, it did not explain the high degree of incineration.

"I'm going out to the car to phone the police," I said.

I was halfway to the vehicle when I paused. I had just passed the opening of another alley when I saw a great shadow sweep across the snow in front of me. Even taking into account the fact that a shadow would've appeared stretched at such an angle, I determined that who-ever made it would have to be over seven feet tall. The silhouette showed a figure in a long cloak-like garment with a hood, carrying some type of staff. There seemed to be a wild crown of bare branches and twigs sticking up from the head and fir branches tied to it so that they stuck out from the shoulders and wound around the sleeves.

I was startled, and only saw for a brief moment as this shadow passed. I spun around...the mouth of the alley was empty but for the windy fluttering snow.

It was a long and bitter night. The snow continued to fall steadily until there were several inches. We had counted as many stray souls as possible before returning to our own safe homes, our cozy beds. Strangely enough, we not only tallied up the number of homeless...there was another count taken, a grim and perplexing one. For on that night, twelve sets of smoky, blackened human bones were found in the snow-haunted alleys of Boston.

THE
SARAH

This was the spot where they found his boat, The Sarah, its hull drumming erratically against the dark wet stones of the shoals. The Atlantic sprawled now as it did then, presiding indifferently, cold and slush-colored, grey as the sky. There had been drizzle that day, a year ago this; it must have brushed against Zach's face like a ghost, or invisible lace. Only gulls witnessed his death, but they saw everything, didn't they, kiting above, or perched on the shore like chess pawns. Were it not for the gulls he would have died alone.

Here, on the Down East coast, the hills were jagged with spruce forest, and small islands floated—puzzle pieces drifting off toward the clean edge of the horizon. All was quiet but for the shush of the tide shrugging against the shore, and the sound of a woman's feet as she stepped softly, so as not to wake the forest.

Sarah moved down from the dirt road and came to a ledge where jumbles of precarious granite stuck out into the surf, a suicide's wharf. The tide was coming in, but it was bored and unthreatening, lapping the base of the projection. This was as close as the young woman could get to the shoals without a boat.

Trees balanced close to the precipice. She stood under these, hugging herself, chill air whipping gold hair. She tried to imagine how it must have been...the shoals, the off-white sky, the drizzle and gulls. One of them had been squatting on his chest when they boarded and found the body. Had he suffered? Did he die as quickly as the doctor claimed? Somehow a year had passed.

Maybe she should have brought flowers to toss into the sea. She had walked miles in the cold, along a winding road with dark woods on either side, the trees offset by snow cover. There hadn't been a great amount of the white stuff this winter, though extended periods of cold reminded everyone that this was still northern New England. The succession of deep freezes had iced over the shallow bays like no one had seen in thirty years, and a boat up in Machiasport suffered buildup so heavy on one side that she tipped, took on water, and went under. No one was on board at the time.

A dirt path that branched away from the road brought Sarah here, offered her this view of the site. With no posy to cast, she bent and stuck her glove into the snow, fumbled until she found a flat, almost circular, stone. It took some effort to free it from the frozen February earth.

Sarah returned her gaze to the ocean and stood holding the stone, silently infusing it with a numb prayer. Gulls called, and crows too. She took a step closer to the edge and let the offering fall; it made a plopping sound and was gone.

The sky looked like it might snow…the weatherman on the radio had made some noncommittal reference to flurries. A breeze was coming over the water, though not enough to cast breakers against the shoals—those stones, ranked in an undulating line, were touched with snow at their most elevated points, the areas where the highest tides could not quite reach. At times, when the tide was up and there was mist on the water, these uneven peaks resembled Nessie, far from her Scotland, with humps breaching the surface.

The shoals extended out from one of those tree-covered puzzle-piece islands that helped to shape the harbor. Sarah pictured her husband's lobster boat bobbing there as if abandoned, rubbing up against the rocks, lonely as the Mary Celeste. Zach, with his love of nautical lore, had become a part of that very mythos, in a sense. She wondered if his ghost would stand mournfully atop the shoals when the moon shone on sea fog, when there was no one there to see. No, it wasn't so darkly romantic as all that—the shoals were incidental, they had not brought The Sarah low, in fact, the boat had only suffered scratches when it wandered to that spot and hovered there, rocking against the outcrop. There was nothing romantic about a twenty-five-year-old man dropping dead from a defective heart.

Funny how she came here, rather than his grave, on the anniversary of his death. But the grave didn't haunt her as this place did—the grave was no more than a repository. While this location was not culpable, *it* happened here. It, like the final and key act in a play that ought to have made sense. But it didn't make sense, and so she imagined it again and again…the man's last hours, what he might have been thinking, or if he had been happy, if death had struck like lightning, if he knew, in that final moment, that she loved him.

The surf was rising, pressing a little further up the base of the ledge where the woman stood. It pulled back, seemed to take a breath, and then swept forward again, slapping and spitting. It went on this way, retreating over a steep incline of stones, riling clumps of rockweed, before sloshing back in.

Sarah stood there a while longer, like a scarecrow, then, turning, muttered softly, "Bye."

«« — »»

Sarah woke sometime after midnight. Sleet was ticking against the windows like a discordant chorus of clocks. A nightlight glowed modestly. She had dreamed of her husband, and the smell of the sea. She reached out to his side of the mattress, to the pillow she had not been able to evict from the bed. Her fingers touched something cold and hard.

Sitting upright, the woman saw the stone. It looked to be the one that she had tossed into the sea, yet it was not so round as she recalled; it looked as if slow chisels of tidal erosion had worried and shaped it. Sarah picked up the heart and pressed it to her own.

THE CRIPPLED GATE

Mrs. O'Brien wasn't quite the same after visiting Marina Panarelli. Her son Dickie knew right away. He arrived home around four o'clock, as he did every workday, having put in his shift at the local plastics plant. He walked into the modest two-story house they shared and called out a hello. Strange—there was no sign of his mother or her wheelchair. Cause for concern. He heard thumping upstairs and his concern escalated. By the time he had grabbed a knife from the kitchen and started up the stairs, his imagination had conjured a number of disturbing scenarios to explain the absence of his mother and the presence of the drumming. Halfway up and he heard her voice; she was singing.

Following a sigh of relief, Dickie opened the door to the vacant chamber that had been the old woman's bedroom before arthritis had consigned her to the chair. Mrs. O'Brien had not been upstairs in years, but there she was in her peach-colored house dress, doing a nice little dance, a jig in fact. She was singing, "He's coming, he's coming, he's coming…"

Dickie stood dumbfounded. He saw something silvery blur past the window behind Mrs. O'Brien. Twenty seconds passed and the object went by again, and though Dickie knew he had only imagined the flying wheelchair, he moved closer to the glass. It swirled around the house a third time and now he saw it break from its orbit and sail off toward Orchard Hill. There was no mistaking; it was indeed a flying wheelchair.

"Damn..." Dickie muttered.

«« — »»

STRANGE SKIES OVER EASTBOROUGH, the headline read. Guy Budge creaked back in his chair, frowned and pressed the backspace button on his keyboard, deleting the line. He tried again: UFOS OVER EASTBOROUGH. No, too mundane, perhaps a touch more color. KEEP YOUR EYES ON THE SKY IN EASTBOROUGH. Budge smiled.

The article that followed bore something of a snide flavor. Budge was a disbeliever in everything except smoking cigarettes two days a year, those days being New Year's day (when puffing masses resolved to quit) and during The Great American Smoke Out; the other days he breathed the grey-smelling air of Worcester, Massachusetts; that seemed to placate any self-destructive impulses. Stories like this gave him the chance to sprinkle a little cynicism into his writing, but when it came to real news, he was a straight arrow.

The Worcester Daily had received a number of calls from Eastborough residents regarding strange objects in the sky. Rather than the conventional saucer sightings, the locals reported seeing crutches and asthma inhalers soaring overhead. One man even witnessed a flying wheelchair.

Guy had spoken with several of these people and while they all seemed normal enough, he was not convinced. Just as he had not been convinced by the nice young couple in Grafton, who claimed their old farm house was haunted, or the hunter who swore he saw a Bigfootesque creature stomping through Eastborough's Cedar Swamp. Guy suspected that his boss Jay secretly admired his acerbic pieces, which would explain why he was given so many of the odd cases.

"Have I got a story for you," Jay said, grinning as he approached Guy Budge's desk in the sprawling pressroom.

Guy looked up; he was forty, his dark hair thinning, his features average but for the eyes, that appeared worried much of the time, perhaps bemused.

"What now, Jay, an Elvis sighting?"

Jay pushed a coffee mug aside and sat on the corner of the desk. "Better. How about a sixteen-year-old girl in a coma who can cure cripples?"

"Groovy."

Jay slipped him a piece of paper that contained a few lines of very basic information. He said, "This kid was in a car accident a couple of months ago; she's in what they call akinetic mutism, a coma-like condition. Apparently they realized that the kid was 'chosen' and gifted with weird powers. Anyway, the kid's mother has turned her home into some kind of a shrine and people are being allowed in to see the girl. One kiss on her forehead and—poof—your hemorrhoids are history."

"Geesh." Guy wagged his head.

"You want this one?"

Of course he did. "Of course I do."

«« — »»

Winter was losing its grip; March drizzle swept into Eastborough, chill and slow from a sky of melting slate. Cars hissed on Route 9 and a waitress with eyes the green of a humid summer freshened Guy's coffee. Her perfume should have been outlawed. Guy nodded his thanks and gazed back out the diner's plate glass and noticed that the drizzle had upgraded to rain.

A beefy cop came jangling in and sat a few stools down. Guy recognized him as Officer North, whom he'd interviewed some months earlier when a man was killed by a car while crossing route 9.

"Officer North…"

The cop turned, serious, then smiled. "Oh, hi."

"Remember me? Guy Budge from the Worcester Daily."

"Sure, how's it going?"

Guy shrugged. "Not too many complaints, and you?"

"Okay. Hey, I liked your article about the UFOs. What brings you to town this time?"

Guy glanced at the window—the rain was insisting on entry. "Marina Panarelli. The comatose teenage healer? You know about that?"

"Oh sure; she's the talk of the town."

"You get any complaints about the flocks converging on the

Panarelli place—I hear it was a quiet neighborhood until this miracle stuff started up?"

"We had one lady complain, until they talked her into going in to see the girl. She came out with her migraines cured."

Guy smiled distrustingly. "Is that so?"

"Yeah," Officer North said, "I think it's great. That kid is curing everything from cancer to warts. It's amazing; I've heard people say she got rid of their arthritis, ulcers, paralyses, even blindness."

"Lepers?" Guy was a devil.

"It's spooky, but in a good way. She's doing more healing than all of those blood-thirsty HMOs put together. Hell, they're offering bonuses at the end of the year to doctors who under-treat patients, to keep costs down. Nice huh? I don't care if it's the power of suggestion or some kind of actual power, but these people are being healed."

Guy nodded patronizingly. He turned to the window. "Was that thunder? A thunderstorm in March, can you believe it? Crazy New England weather."

«« — »»

The rain made strange music on black umbrellas. Cars were lined up like it was a graduation party, the line of people going out the door like it was the wake of someone popular. Guy had to park some distance away. He noted his surroundings; a pleasant neighborhood of Colonials and Victorians in moderate repair. A nice middle-class street. He took his place at the end of the line.

A round man in his fifties turned and smiled. He urged Guy to move closer so as to share his umbrella. He seemed an ordinary man. The others were also regular people, some old, some young. They all looked hopeful, eager. A woman carrying a screaming baby was admitted into the modest white house.

"What have you got?" the big fellow asked.

"Ulcers," Guy lied, although he wondered at times.

"I got a tumor," the man stated, pointing to somewhere on his expansive midsection.

Guy nodded soberly. "Say, do you know any of the details about Marina's accident?"

"Why yes, I believe I do. You haven't heard?"

Rain on the man's umbrella sounded like some garbled, unintelligible language.

"All I know," Guy replied, "is that she was in an accident a couple of months ago."

"Yes sir, yes indeed, a freak accident. Do you remember that mummified baby they found over in one of those A-rab countries, buried with a bunch of gold offerings and jewels?"

Guy squinted. "Oh, yes, I think I heard something about that; they called him the Squid King because of those deformities. Thousands of years old, right, but very well preserved?"

"Bingo! They flew it over here and toured it around from museum to museum for a few months. Well, it was snowing and Rosa—she's Marina's mom—had just picked up Marina and a friend; I guess they'd spent the afternoon at the Worcester Science Museum, right? So, they went to drive away and some idiot stepped out into the road…Rosa had to swerve; she lost control of the car and it slammed right into the back of the truck that was unloading that little mutant mummy. The car ruptured the crate that the thing was in and it went flying. I heard it did some flips that would've made an Olympic diver green with envy. Marina went flying too, straight through the windshield. Freakishly enough, she ended up sprawled on the hood of the car with that dead baby on top of her and one of its strange appendages down her throat."

Guy flinched as someone screamed and he saw a young woman running out of the house joyously waving a painful-looking metal leg brace in the rain above her head. People applauded.

"That's how it happened," the storyteller concluded. "It wasn't brain damage from the crash; it was that mummy's limb down her throat that blocked the air to her brain and put her in the state she's in now. Funny, though, 'cause it was a miracle really, if you think about it."

The wind found Guy's neck and he shivered. "Yeah, a miracle."

《《—》》

Incense, dimness, spooky paintings of Christ, taped organ music from somewhere, with an undercurrent of hissing from cheap speakers. It was like a bad funeral. Guy was inside the Panarelli residence. Rosa, both mother and conductor, orchestrated people down a short hall into her daughter's bedroom. Guy thought of the dark interiors of freak show tents at the Brockton Fair of his youth. Rosa was pleasingly plump, a warm, dark basket of faith, the name Jesus quick and frequent at her lips. She had that spark of belief in her eyes, or was it the candles?

"Just kiss her head," Rosa instructed, "and the Lord's healing will be upon thee."

Thee? Guy smirked. Pul-ease!

Suddenly there came the triumphant sounds of another satisfied customer. Guy thought the only thing missing was a collection plate. Soon it was his turn. He glanced back at the rapturous Rosa who stood to one side with her sentient toddler daughter and serious eighteen-year-old son flanking. Apparently there was no Mr. Panarelli. An old woman with squirrel-colored hair had gotten behind Guy and now her bony hands were on his back, pushing him into Marina's room.

The room was dark. A figure lay on a bed beneath a grey blanket. Jesus, painted on velvet, stared out of the shadows, his eyes twitching with candlelight. The air was stale, and while Guy was not prone to claustrophobia, he suddenly found himself touched with sympathy for those who were. One by one the broken people filed past, bending over the girl before moving out an opposite door and on out of the house.

Guy Budge came within feet of Marina Panarelli. He could hear hissing and gurgles—medical machines stationed behind the dark dressing screen? Marina might have been asleep. She looked peaceful, pretty even, with rosaries like the ocean-worn skeletons of snakes left on her lap.

The friendly man in front of Guy crossed himself, bent, and kissed the girl's clammy head. He rose up weeping. "Praise the Lord! He's coming!" On his way out, the heavy man did a little jig that jostled the velvet Christ.

Guy's turn. He hovered above Marina, inexplicably repelled. Her mouth was slightly ajar, her great lashes of crow-darkness folded. Her flesh looked cool, so close, as he slowly lowered his head over hers. He felt her breath on his face and in this dizzy moment, with her pale forehead waiting, he imagined that he saw into her dark and quiet dream. There was a peppering of stars and broken worlds and something in the darkness moved, or was it an echo? What did he hear? He felt his soul brace inside, afraid it might fall into the blackness with her. Guy pulled away and rushed out into the rain.

《《——》》

"It doesn't have your usual spark," Jay observed, pacing in his office, in a grey building in grey downtown Worcester. He was carrying a tear sheet.

Guy was slumped in a leather chair pondering an unlit cigarette. "It's not my best work."

Jay mumbled, re-reading to himself. "You made your visit to the coma kid sound like one of those fun house tunnels, with the weird mirrors and uneven floors."

"Well, it was a rather carnival-like scene. Disturbing. People are such sheep, so desperate. It's scary."

Guy thought of the sounds and told himself it had just been the sound of the girl's empty stomach growling. It had to be that, he told himself.

Jay put the paper down on his desk, folded his arms and studied his friend. "What's wrong, Guy?"

"Nothing, Jay."

"We have to revitalize you, my friend. Maybe you need more stimulation in your life; what happened to the fiery romance you had going with that legal secretary?"

Guy sighed. "That fiery romance is now a tepid association. But it's not that, Jay. Maybe I just need better material…"

Tall, blond, aristocratic looking (some might say) Jay grinned. "I've got a goody for you. It would make the perfect side bar to this Sleeping Beauty thing."

"You're the boss."

"Well, it seems that the people who supposedly have been healed by Marina have made something of an impromptu shrine in Eastborough…"

"A shrine," Guy repeated. He stuck the cigarette in his mouth.

"What's with the butt?"

"I stole it."

"You're not going to smoke that are you?"

"I haven't decided."

《《——》》

Orchard Hill was no longer an orchard. It rose solemnly, steeply; a dirt road went up it and the wind went down it. Teens often parked where the trees once grew, for the privacy more than the view, which, in a time when New England wilderness was being gobbled up by developers, was surprisingly scenic, tenuously unspoiled.

Guy could see the recently erected structure from some distance, silhouetted up on the hill. He crushed a cigarette in the ashtray, parked and climbed out. The day was warm and sunlight gleamed on the strange arch-like monument. It was a jumble of abandoned wheelchairs, canes and walkers, oxygen machines and crutches. There was even a glass eye peering at him from out the chrome and shadows.

"Geesh," Guy whispered.

It reminded him of the trilithons of Stonehenge or some kind of jagged overgrown door frame. A gate?

Guy took several pictures of the thing and the wind made strange sounds as it found its way through the skeletal metal.

《《——》》

The healed were abundant in downtown Eastborough, where Guy had gone seeking interviews. Outside the coffee shop, outside the stone library, outside the brick town hall. They sauntered and smiled blissfully. Attendance was down in local churches, their flocks thinning. Marina's expanding body of benefactors were transferring their loyalties, gathering to pray at the Orchard Hill wheelchair shrine.

Guy found himself avoiding the no-longer-handicapped. They made him nervous for some reason or other. He was wearing a gun under his sports coat now, a small dark Smith and Wesson .38. He usually reserved the gun for when his duties placed him in the less wholesome sections of Worcester. He had taken to wearing it continuously after his visit to the Panarelli house, though he could not quite say why.

He had tried to dismiss the growling he had heard, close to the girl in her dark room. It was easy enough to blame that on her empty stomach. But the other sensations had been even more unnerving. It was as if he had tuned in to her crippled mind and seen something waiting there in unborn blackness. But why hadn't any of the others felt the same horror? Why did he dash out in a cold sweat while they flung their crutches aside and pranced around like they were in a Riverdance audition?

Perhaps he possessed a certain sensitivity that the general public lacked. Once, while doing a story in Salem, he had interviewed a psychic. She had said something about him having a certain shine to him. He said it was just a sunburn. A card carrying disbeliever, Guy had always belittled the strange coincidences and synchronicities that had followed him through life.

There were times when he had questioned the idea of having a peculiar gift of perception, like that time in high school when he had slipped a small mirror under Jenny Crosby's desk…somehow he had sensed that she wasn't wearing panties. He had always had an uncanny knack for knowing where the Easter Bunny (his dad) had hidden the chocolate eggs. Then there was the time he was home alone and the bully from two houses down knocked at the door…he just knew there was a flaming bag of poop out there waiting for him on the doorstep.

But most unsettling of all, was that Halloween night when he'd been awakened by a strange belch-like sound in the darkness and opened his eyes to see the image of his Uncle Todd, standing at the foot of his bed with a slippery Macintosh stuffed in his kisser. He latter discovered that the vision had appeared at the exact time that his beloved uncle had drowned in a drunken apple-bobbing mishap.

Humbug! But why the gun? Why was he afraid to close his eyes and see the peaceful face of a comatose girl?

《《—》》

In the coming weeks Marina's popularity grew. Guy felt guilty for this, wondering if the article he had written had been little more than publicity for the freakshow going on in that little white house on Willard Street. Other papers had to share the blame, however, for they too picked up on the craze. A local cable station had done a spot on the miracle-girl and there were rumors that a major television network was considering featuring her on one of its "news" programs. While reaction was mixed and Guy was glad to see some people horrified and disgusted at the exploitation factor, the lines outside the Panarelli house were growing day by day.

While Guy was not at all surprised to see other papers touting tales of the Marina phenomenon, he felt more than a competitive jolt when, walking past a newstand, he saw an enemy paper's headline proclaim: COMA GIRL PREGNANT.

«« — »»

In Shrewsbury, adjacent to Worcester, Guy Budge and a dust-colored cat named Olsen rented a small east-facing Cape. It was early April and the grass had turned green where he stood in the dark, smoking a cigarette, gazing heavenward, his cordless phone pressed to an ear. Lately it bothered him to look at the stars, small and bright, and the sky that seemed too big.

He was talking to Officer North at the Eastborough Police. "It had to be Marina's brother," Guy was saying.

"I'd hate to think that," the policeman returned.

"Come on, North, it had to be. Here's this kid; he's eighteen and he's in this fanatically religious house where his raging hormones are knotted up with holy repression and, conveniently, in the next room, there's a sixteen-year-old female body just lying there for the taking. Sister or not, the temptation must be immense. Besides, comatose girls don't say 'no'."

The cop groaned. "That's sick, Guy."

Guy saw the silvery stroke of a meteor. "Absolutely sick, but it happens. Hell, half the human males you meet on the street are likely to have enacted some kind of incestuous abuse. We're just base mammals beneath our loafers and ties, my friend."

"I hope you're wrong. I really hope you're wrong, Guy, but I have to admit he is the first name on our suspect list. The mother had a fit when we even hinted at the possibility and when we talked to the kid, he seemed pretty darn believable. He insists he never touched her. The mother says it's a miracle; she swears Marina is still a virgin. We'll see; a doctor's going over to examine her tomorrow."

«« — »»

The wind had its eager, colorless hands on the trees. The robins were out and brave flowers tried to paint a pretty world, but Guy Budge was not fooled. It was stop and go out of Worcester, onto Route 9, battling trucks, and soccer moms in their gleaming vans. The wind slapped his car from side to side.

He was supposed to be in the city covering a pit bull attack, but instead he found himself headed for Eastborough, although he had talked Jay into relieving him of having to cover anything related to Marina Paranelli. He passed a billboard for an HMO, over which someone had spray painted: THE SAVIOR IS COMING.

The news had come over the wire. It was big news. A doctor had examined the pregnant comatose girl. Her hymen was indeed intact, it had been reported, in so many words, making her pregnancy a complete medical mystery. "Looks like the brother's off the hook," Guy muttered to himself.

He drove into Eastborough proper with its pleasant residential neighborhoods—white houses, green lawns. Willard Street was congested with parked vehicles and a dense crowd stood outside of the Panarelli house. Guy felt his guts tense at the sight of the place and he had to resist the sudden urge to turn and drive away.

The man parked the car and mumbled to himself, "Immaculate conception, huh? There must be some explanation..."

His eyes looked more worried than ever. He put his left arm in a fake sling ala Ted Bundy, and proceeded on foot to the back of the line. It was a long wait.

Guy's heart ached for the sick and disadvantaged waiting to kiss the girl's head. He ached for her too, for her tragic mishap and the fiasco it had furnished. But he was starting to believe that something in that house was actually mending people. How could he not believe when there was the simple before and after proof of blind men seeing and cripples walking? But why were they being fixed?

It was not Jesus that Guy had heard when he had leaned close to Marina; there was no name for those sounds. Unbeknownst to the restored and faithful followers, their savior was not The Christ returned. But what was it and how would they serve it, once it arrived? Who would stop it? Guy felt the cool weight of his revolver against his ribs.

The shades were drawn to keep the house dark, the air misty with incense, humming with organ music. Rosa Panarelli was greeting the visitors, instructing them, ushering them along. Guy's arm was hot in its sling, the palm-sized cassette recorder slick in his palm. There were only four people in front of him now. The hunched old man behind him was wheezing.

Guy and Rosa made eye contact.

"Hello, Mrs. Panarelli."

"Oh, hello," she spoke pleasantly.

"Tell me, have you any idea when the baby will come?"

"Why yes. The savior will come in September."

"September," Guy repeated.

Rosa's warm hand was on his shoulder and she was moving him along. "Just kiss her forehead and the Lord's blessing will be upon you," she said.

Guy smiled uncomfortably and nodded. He turned and stepped into the dark bedroom where a figure lay mannequin-like on a bed. A father lifted his small boy, bald from chemotherapy, so that he could kiss the girl. The boy placed a crude crayon drawing of Jesus on Marina's chest; it made Guy think of the shroud of Turin.

The old man behind Guy was rasping, the velvet Christ was glaring, all the heat in his body flew up into his head and spun. He was beside her now and she was impassive, waxen, a large breathing doll. Her eyes were closed, her mouth slightly open. Guy stared at the mound of her belly as it rose and fell beneath the covers. He bent closer, his lips over her head as he pressed the small hidden tape recorder to the side of her belly.

He closed his eyes and her dream was there—vast and dark and waiting. The stars were hungry. Half an inch separated his mouth from her skull. He wavered, dizzy; he felt the baby kick and drew the recorder away. He pulled back up and in feigned fervor exclaimed, "I'm healed! The savior is coming!"

《《—》》

Something about September, but what? Why would the savior be born in September? Guy gripped the wheel of his Pontiac with one hand and worked the little recorder with the other. He played back what the machine had heard in Marina's belly. It was the million stars screaming. Guy shuddered. A million hungry stars were screaming, calling to be wakened. But why September? Because it was nine months after the Squid King had one of its vile tendrils stuffed down Marina Panarelli's throat.

Guy clicked the recorder off. He knew he had to kill the girl.

《《—》》

May and June and July came, and August with flies as big as raisins. There were wide summer days with heat soaking up from the south and thunder stomping after dark. Guy was chain-smoking now and the calendar was passing under his feet. How long could he put it off? What price would he pay for aborting that great horror? At best he'd be imprisoned, providing he was not torn apart by the flock. How ironic, he thought…a martyr's death.

What would become of those that Marina had healed, Guy wondered, spinning the cylinder on his dark little .38. If he was to kill her, would they be released from the healing spell? He thought about the children that would die of leukemia, of the blind returned to their worlds of sound, of bodies pained and defective, of hopelessness and pain. But what would be the alternative? If the healed were to revert to their broken states, they would be martyrs, the sacrificed, and better some die and suffer than all perish to feed the hungry stars. It was definitely a lesser of two evils situation.

It was the night before September and already the first sly yellows were crippling leaves. The days had shortened, the sun sleeping longer, waking later. Crows called the harvest in with craven black flags.

Quietly wheeling his car onto Willard Street, Guy Budge was surprised to find that there was no crowd outside the small white Paranelli homestead. The house was dark but for a light in a first floor bedroom. He had expected a great throng there, awaiting the September birth. There was no one. He parked. Crickets sang him to the door.

The front door was unlocked. Simple enough. He opened it and peered into blackness. He felt the family cat brush his legs as it slipped out. He did not remember whether they had a cat or not; perhaps it was a new addition.

The gun came out, its handle both smooth and checkered in his damp hand. He knew the small hallway, he knew which door to go to. The carpeting was soft beneath him, almost slick in spots. One hand found the knob, turned; the pistol dragged him into the room.

Guy gasped. He was too late. Marina was at last freed from her purgatory, broken on the red and white bed. The newborn had not made a graceful exit from her as it entered the world. The midwife was crumpled alongside the bed. How had it done that to her face? Where was Rosa? Where was the baby?

Quickly, back into the hall, flashlight from his pocket, light splashing. The carpet slick, wild dark patterns to the next room. Rosa Panarelli face down, wet. The older brother in the next room; he had tried to get out the window. Flashlight stark, bright on dark runny walls. Into the kitchen—no sign of it yet. How big was it? How fast? Gun first to the kitchen. The little sister, ruined.

Guy sagged against the refrigerator; magnets fell, clattered on the floor; a child's crayon drawing flapped down, close to spatters. His eyes followed it down and widened. He bent and picked it up, shined the light on it.

The child had drawn a squid-like blob outside of a crude house. There were dotted lines rambling away from the house like roads on a map. The lines led to a crude hill and a familiar shape—the monument on Orchard Hill. An arrow pointed through the crayon gate and on the other side of that gate hovered a huge cloud-like planet of Medusa limbs.

Guy looked up and muttered, "The screaming stars will wake when it goes through the gate."

The drawing dropped from his fingers and fluttered down into the blood.

«« —»»

Screeching off Mill Pond Road, the Pontiac carved a cloud out of the dirt as it made the corner onto the adjacent trail. The .38 slid across the passenger seat. Guy snarled, stomped the gas, fishtailed. The hill came up in the headlights.

The sloping sides were covered with people—the restored faithful in great numbers. They were not at the Panarelli house because they were here waiting at the gate for the real birth—the birth of an ancient god.

The followers were lined up on either side of the road that led up the hill, shouting, shaking their fists as the car growled up the slope, headlights glaring on the small dark shape that was slurping along like the head of a string mop. Only feet to go before it reached the gate.

"No!" Guy raged.

The car shot to the top of the hill—he braced, aimed for one of the pillars. A jumble of wheelchairs filled the windshield, luminous in the headlights. Closer and closer—Guy could see the odd prosthetic limb jutting out and Depends stuffed like mortar between false teeth and orthopedic sneakers. It was not the gate to heaven and there was no sign of Saint Peter.

The car hit hard, the gate broke, rained down in small and large pieces and the babe was beneath, screeching. The windows that survived the crash were shattered by its cry.

It was that simple. The evil had been felled without the use of ancient incantations, without magic circles and dusty tomes. There were no bubbling potions or mysterious symbols drawn in blood...all it took was a panicking reporter's gas-pedal foot and an uninsured Pontiac to save the universe. The monster stuck one of its appendages in the air in a gesture that might have been construed as obscene, then went limp beneath the rubble.

Guy was stunned, slumped. Steam was rasping from the accordion metal of his car. He blinked his brain out of the mist and saw the ruin. He heard the horrified voices of the milling devotees.

"It's dead!"

"He killed it!"

"Get him!"

"Kill him!"

Guy pushed against his door but it was jammed. He reached for the gun but felt only broken bits of windshield like glass teeth. The mob was surrounding the car, moving in; a grimacing old man stamping toward the smashed window. Guy pulled back but they were nearing the passenger window too. Then the old man stopped. He reached out and groped at the air. Blind. Guy saw a woman stagger and fall, her legs failing. Outside the passenger window a young man went rigid, tilted and fell down like a board, his body once again paralyzed.

"Where's my wheelchair?" Mrs. O'Brien cried from the ground.

"What am I doing here?" another asked.

One man was calling for his oxygen and a young girl was having an asthma attack.

The hill was covered with cripples and people carrying tumors like time bombs, sick and suffering people, a tragic assortment of the blind and broken. Some of those with useful limbs climbed over the rubble of the crippled gate to help the poor man out of his car.

«« — »»

Sometime in October, Guy Budge went back to Orchard Hill. He watched as the sun floated down behind the colorful trees and as dusk blurred up in deep watercolor blues. The crows went silent and the stars came, soft like tears in candlelight.

He took out a cigarette but decided not to light it. Instead, he reached back behind the passenger seat to stuff it into the crinkled grocery bag he kept for trash. A nearly full pack of cigarettes followed.

He was still haunted by guilt and while he did not expect that it would dissipate soon, it made him feel somewhat better to think …maybe, just maybe he had saved the world.

THE SEPTEMBER FAIR

September came with narrow days, with quickening dusk, with fox-red sunset and crows. There were ribbons of gooseflesh down the spine and moccasin—soft leaves under flaking maples. The sky, flat over unexpected breezes, closer to the west, predicted a smooth pumpkin moon. Slate-colored rain balmed the scorched fields and the last urgent memories were made.

I perched behind August and weighed the long days, like blurred dreams scrawled on greasy paper napkins. Rumbling yellow buses exhumed childhood dread and my heart flew up like a kite in my chest.

September also brought the fair. It was Saturday and Sunday with the month's eyes closing when the gypsy clutter of trailers and tents crowded the cowless grass. It was a modest spectacle of rickety stands and fly-freckled picnic tables set in crooked rows across sun-flattened fields. This was summers funeral of slow blue jean mourners, of mothers towing tots, of homemade pies and handmade wreaths and somber joy to mock the clotting cold.

There was a yard sale, junkyard, open—aired museum of tables in a row, where round bearded men gloated over altars of archaic tools—from rust—reaping pitchforks and antique metal shapes that few could identify, to reverently preserved disembodied coughing steam engines. Bucolic men milled, with pocketed hands and boyish eyes, or sat like kings presiding over their oily treasures.

I moved through the fair with its noises and colors, nameless amidst the languid flow of spectators. My nose feasted on quilted scents, the bronze air of pomace by an ancient cider press, weathered and trampled weeds, the crowding invisible colors of dung and sizzling hot dogs, of hearth-entrusted baked goods whispering of kitchens and soapy—handed grandmothers.

Plastic cups crunched like pinecones beneath the many feet and workhorses with clovered hooves tugged jostling wagons packed with day-trippers and scratchy blocks of hay. There were cigarette stubs like dead hornets in matted grass and close strangers mingling perfume and sweat and beer-tainted laughter.

A willow of a girl with bored rain-colored eyes hovered over a flock of pumpkins, her twig arms crossed on a budded chest, the raisin dark of her hair spilled and restless. She half-watched, half-dreamed, half-leaned on skinny legs, sad perhaps, as her summer blood slowed, or mourning the loss of a fleet summer love, her half-broken heart a mumble of drowning thorns.

Younger children spilled through a forest of legs; giggles of flesh, dappled with ketchup, smiling mustard-smeary smiles and damp ice cream beards. Their stubby hands were like pale sticky starfish towing balloons or clutching jagged sugar cones.

I moved among tables of produce and crafts—folk trinkets with warm subdued tones, embroidered samplers, wreaths that breathed dusty lavender and thyme. Flattened fork wind chimes rocked in icy chatter as I trailed behind my dowsing nose, following taunting wafts of apple crisp.

In the old barn stood three women and five stoves, the latter being antiques smoothed in skull—white porcelain. The women were as old as the stoves and round as baskets with faces of wicker and hair like silver cotton candy. The shadows bore the darkness and aroma of moist coffee grounds and draped about the place like the wings of huge birds, hiding on the rafters.

I took my place in line, my belly full of spider webs and my mouth just as dry. A spatula rasped across a wide square pan the color of a slate grave and the golden crisp cowered in a corner until it was scooped up and slid onto a paper plate. I was behind a stout man with a head like an egg and folds of pink flesh above his shirt collar. He ordered a splat of ice cream to top his dessert and a plastic cup's measure of piss—gold cider. His voice was like charcoal and those sags of flesh at the back of his head moved when he spoke, like auxiliary lips.

The serving ladies seemed somehow younger, costumed as they were in the garb of the 1800s. Sparrow-brief flickers of youth lied in blue squints and cobwebby giggles—old women giggling like grey water over chill stones and September spiders shrouding ice-colored moths in the dark wings of shadow above. But sneakers poked from under their tented skirts, squashing a constellation of crumbs, and they smelled like attics and old newspaper and brittle flesh and the bureau's lowest drawer. The one who served me smiled a thousand and ten tiny yellow teeth, her bonnet's lace like a nimbus of web about her cracking face.

With a pirate's grin, I slipped off with my coveted feast, back out into the copious air. The baked mash of apples melted like sunlight on my tongue, the juice of Eden and Johnny Appleseed sweat waltzing with the pink.

I gazed upon my fellow fair-goers, the feral boys with snotty sneers, ball caps and stiff hairless limbs like rolled newspaper. They gibbon-swaggered for clots of cat-prowl girls with mirror-conscious manes and severe lipstick. The girls were aloof and desired and full of their own nasty laughter, bouncing off each other's rubber elbows, casting quick side glances to count their share of stares.

I drifted my coffee-sipping, crisp-crunching way east past the food stands with their steam skirling and hand-painted signs and flies like b-b holes on fluttery tent walls, along the aisle of hissing engines and men with tattooed flab. Men with war stories in their eyes, with inbred grins and ankhs of sweat staining their T-shirts.

Where the field ended and the trees began and an incorrigible fringe of goldenrod warped to the whims of breeze, a dark pickup held a mass of silvery pipes and adored black metal. It was a steam-driven organ ghosting the air with a hum and sardonic kite-high pitches, music both medieval and tacky for an invisible merry-go-round of sulfur-breathing horsies all polish and bone. It was the sound of carnivals and funerals, of waltzing skeletons and funhouse mirrors.

A soggy scarecrow of a man tended the thing, black leafy hand-prints on his blue overalls and the chestnut rag of a dog at his feet. He was old and his eyes were staples in a face of scrimshaw. I smiled at the psychotically merry peals of sound, picturing the music as a black praying mantis. He caught my eye and nodded, his rattle of a laugh bloodless and his tongue like the head of an adder tucked in damp blackness.

That's when I turned and saw the girl. She was a windy dress with a head and arms of lazy milk and hair that dug black fingers into the wind, climbing the sky behind her. Cotton billowed about the sunlight; she was swift-legged, slow and fast and floating through the moon-tugged tides of her own salty garments. A costume fib of the 1800s. She did not see my face hanging over my coffee cup, my pivoting stupor as lightning thundered down through my chest, counting the organs with rough fingers.

Her face was silk with an upturned nose and conch-pink lips under caramel eyes, shy beneath lids like petals. The dark perfume of her hair flamed at the bright air with cracks and wisps over her forehead and dyed the drunken torrents behind her. She was but the moment, the full skirt forming and shriveling and sail-wide again as she reached the field's trampled center and was gone in a restless, spreading crowd of onlookers.

My feet were my brain as I stepped in her steps and breathed where her passing had softened the air. Was that lilac from the chalk of her neck, essence dabbed behind ears where the taste of salt shaded beneath licorice hair? Was it the bright tumult of May flowers pressed in her flesh like scrapbook blooms, whispering her fading path through a September afternoon?

The steam engine knifed the air and a crow counted three and I felt the coffee like gravel in my gut. Shoulder-deep confusion slowed my pace, past the fizzling food tents, past the trinket stands and tables where vase-shaped women doted over rich pies and shameless cairns of cookies. The golden smell of pumpkin pies blurred the smell of the girl. Then the air was greasy with popcorn and sharp with chips of raw onion shriveling in the sun and the girl was only the black of her hair flitting between bobbing heads and upward beards of cigarette smoke.

One plum-colored kiss and the summer could die. Was that so much to ask? A scribble of lips for the diary of paper napkins? One memory to thumb and press against my pale heart when September, October and November hung clouds of horsehair plaster? Would one kiss be a crime?

At length I saw what the crowd, in cow-silent, sheep-fidgeting milling, sought. It was a parade of slow, chugging tractors. Fat men and scrawny boys perched on rattly, clanging, hissing machines, smokily carving a great circle about the grounds. They traced a puttering history with knobby black tires, their beasts flat, blunt, tall, skeletal, old and tapping like tin, new with bright paint and coughing out cabbages of smoke. A spotted dog trotted alongside, smiling his crazy tongue for the wind. Excusing myself, I wormed through the worshippers, and broke across the clunky caravan's path. An ogre with muscles like heaped gingerroot and tattoos the blurry blue of juniper berries mumbled boozy disapproval at my sacrilege. Something small brushed my thighs and quick liquid darkened my trousers and a squirt gun receded like a plastic cobra behind a warm wall of bodies.

Safe on the opposite side, I despaired. My nose groped the air for the sweet ribbon of her perfume. The apple crisp breezed to betray me. With scanning haste, I ducked past a straw man who leaned like a drunkard and stone walls spidered with branches of bittersweet. Two maples, then three, then four went by, my heart whirling hot through my head. Spiny fists of light punched holes in the leafy ceiling while acorns ground like teeth in the quick sleep beneath my feet.

The house floated up from behind the trees, two story walls the color of shadow and blood supporting a steep grey roof and a hornets' nest like a crumbling paper breast. Chilly windows stretched and shone like grave-slates slick with rain. The never bright herb bed and near-fallen stone walls echoed the sagging grace of the old wooden relic.

TOURS FOR TWO DOLLARS the painted sign read.

I saw her! Her skirt, at least. A white blur flashed around the corner of the house, indistinct material like smoke behind an idling car. At once there was blood and thunder in my legs and a map of clumsy shadows whisking beneath.

I thought I saw her through a window, liquid and lovely with pearl-smooth face between midnight hair and arms inviting with serpentine brine. I thought I saw her eyes in flight—two small, startled caramel-colored birds.

I panted my hello, having raced around the corner a second short of collision with a hunched old figure in colonial guise. Up she smiled with a cherry pit stare and too-perfect teeth the white of a cue ball. Out she reached, a hand like mandrake with wax paper flesh thin over thread-blue ribbons to accept my extended dollars.

The house was an historic site, the woman explained, her dried worm lips squirming around that mouth of full of dice, but I scarce could hear for the blood pounding up the stairs in my chest, a thousand spiders boiling in my feet. The girl, with her milk and ink and unborn kisses and smooth tactile secrets, was in the house and I had to find her.

Quick came the clack on the steps, the creak of the door, the hall still and shadowed. Two hundred years had ground to dust, and hung grey in the copper air where shadows formed the shapes of rooms. The first was all corners with broad board floors and colt-legged tables and flat doilies like great sooty snowflakes and a comatose sofa with moth-burns and glimpses of stuffing pale and yellow as dead rabbits.

I was alone in sagging sepia, with dumb clocks and calcified teacups and a spider across the ceiling like pitch from a squirrel's paw. I shook, full of scalding veins, my chest clanging like a blacksmith's shop, and my eyes without time for citrine faces framed behind glass smoky as quartz.

On into the next room with its curtains like nightshirts and bottles on the sill spilling green and brown shadows and the tart memory of wood smoke black on the stone lip of a drafty fireplace. Where was the girl?

Murmurs towed me into an adjoining chamber. A middle-aged guide with a puffy bonnet was prattling local history to nodding explorers beneath the dried smoky-green of herbs. The room was half hearth, half shadow, more past than present, a quaint clutter of kettles and skillets and hair-cracked porcelain. Where was the girl?

Soft fluttery steps whimpered across the ceiling.

I made quick to find the stairs, and was quickly sad for a paper sign was strung across them warning of incomplete renovations—no visitors allowed upstairs. Two hundred heartbeats later, having stared up the narrow stairs with criminal stirrings at taut reigns, I took the first step. A step as slow as a candle's tear. Up I went on planks worn white by tempests of child-feet and reticent fatherly strides and the weight of plush berry-cheeked mothers. I was up through the tilted chamber, a railing pouring smooth as syrup beneath the sweat of my palm.

Lilac enclosed my head when I reached the uppermost step. She was close. I was full of hungry trembles, breathing the cloying vestige till it fevered in my veins and wove slow comets through the dark rooms of my heart. I hurtled down a vestibule behind her swooning air and saw as one half-sees, her milk splash of fleeting skirt through the doorway and into a room. I heard her footfalls flutter, then a thump like the start of a heart.

I caught myself and slowed, and stopped with one foot in the room and one breath knifing from my throat in a terrible exclamation. It was a naked room, a bedchamber without a bed or any other stick of furniture, save for the strange skeletal simulations of web and shadow. The walls and ceiling were blank as pocked toast and the floor littered with crumbs of plaster. There was no girl.

A small caramel-colored bird lay on the floor beneath a cracked window, dead in its shadow, its shadow adrift in a sallow pond of September light. I knelt and for the first time in my life, my knees creaked. With fingers numb and pale as candles, I lifted the little bird. It crumbled in my hands and down rained her ashes like the shadows of snow.

SHADOW PAINTING

"I'm so scared," Julie whispered against the warm black mass of the Scottish terrier. The fur was damp from tears, the skin along the back rippling involuntarily at the soft nudging of the young woman's nose as if to repel some unwelcome insect intruder. "I'm scared."

The deep internal vacuum Julie felt herself falling into was not unexplored territory. It was a realm of scars, and memories like murals. The impression of her first day at school was there, the imagery still vivid. A strange brick building of harsh angles and cold dark windows, and Mom's maroon Oldsmobile driving off down the street, leaving Julie standing there small and alone. It had felt as if her intestines were tied to it like *just married* streamers dangling from the back bumper, dragging across the pavement. Her sense of familiarity and security was yanked out of her as she watched through her tears when Mom's car reached the end of the street, turned and vanished.

She had walked onto the lawn of the school with a rumpled brown lunch bag clenched in hand. In frustration, she had hurled the plump bag at one of the trees; the sack had fallen on the ground, its belly-like bulge torn and the pale corner of a sandwich bag poking out. She cried all the harder at this, empathizing with the poor discarded lunch, and after her mother had lovingly packed it.

The next mural displayed another big alien building, similar unfriendly angles, glossy bright corridors filled with a stingingly clean antiseptic stench. Auntie Karen all but dragging her by the hand. "Mommy, Mommy…"

Death was an unfathomable concept at the age of six, a dark intangible fairytale thing that only happened to strangers, not her Mommy. How could Mommy have abandoned her like that? How could Auntie Karen just drive her away and leave Mommy lying silent back in that vast scary building with all those strangers?

Julie went to live with her aunt and uncle in a new town with new schools. She hovered on the fringes of peer cliques—other children were disparate and rowdy creatures—she was timid and solemn. She hated recess, the playground like a great tar shadow where other kids formed a colorful noisy fog. She did not belong.

Auntie Karen gave her a puppy when she turned eight. He was a Scottish terrier, a compact and energetic little beast. She called him Shemp. They adored and depended on each other, forming a world no one else could touch. He would run yipping down the sidewalk to greet her when she climbed off the school bus. She would ride around with the pup in her bike basket, his paws up on the silver metal, snout shoved out like a missile, eyes wide with delight. Over the years, as sporadic friends came and went, Shemp remained a constant, his unquestioned love for her never faltering.

Now Roger had left her, though he maintained that he still wanted to be friends. For six months he had been telling her that he loved her. For six months he had teased her for being so quiet, for wearing boring clothes, for reading. He even complained that her breasts were too small.

"Fuck you, Roger," Julie choked. Shemp squirmed out from where the woman was curled around him and he poked his head from under the blankets. His sad brown eyes peered through scraggily bangs and a coarse tongue caressed the tears from Julie's face.

«« —»»

The face was black and white, the deep-set eyes caught in lazy contemplation, the mouth drawn in a reserved sneer, as if the man in the picture found the world he was thinking about contemptible. He was enigmatic.

116

"His last painting," Julie noted aloud, "a self portrait."

Kim looked over her friend's shoulder at the magazine.

"Oh, he's ugly."

"He is not. He's artistic looking."

Half of the man's face was in shadow, the cheeks cutting in darkly, left eye nestled in a palm of blackness, the nose outlined harshly. His hair was longish and untamed, black.

"He's ugly," Kim maintained.

"Unconventional. Moody," Julie protested softly.

The other pages contained more photographs of Ryan Burns' black and white oil paintings. There was a plane wreck, a hypothermic homeless man huddled dead in a murky alley, a man slumped in the front seat of a car with coils of dark liquid snaking down his neck from a gangland-style bullet wound. Across the top of one page Artist Magazine had arranged several portraits, also black and white.

"Oh," Kim said sarcastically, "Look, he did something normal. Faces. Hey, she's even smiling!"

Julie grinned and tried not to sound too defensive. "Those are murder victims he did from photos for a collection called In Happier Times."

"Christ, the guy was obsessed with death. Must've been a Scorpio. Yeah, he looked like a Scorp."

Kim walked over to a window and peered through the blinds at the street below. Cars hissed through September drizzle. Even in the dull light of an overcast day her fairness contrasted with Julie's deeper hues. Kim was what Roger would have considered an ideal female…long, full-breasted, blond, blue-eyed, with an enticing burst of mane and revealing clothing to boot. Julie was short, moon-faced, with tense brown eyes and a discontented pout.

The two roommates complimented each other in tastes as well as looks. Julie loved the somber tones of cello music and PBS television programs, while Kim craved loud music she could air-fuck to on a dance floor, and reality programs. Kim was a business major and Julie, of course, was an arts major.

Shemp wandered into the living room of their off-campus flat, eyes glossy with cataracts, his shaggy coat dry and streaked silver. He sniffed the carpet, found Julie's scent, and traced her to the couch. Images were merely blurs to the old dog.

"Jump," Julie said.

Shemp stood there looking up and waited for her to reach down and lift him. His jumping days were over. Julie adjusted herself so that he could curl up in her lap, where he near-instantly fell asleep. Julie delved back into the magazine article.

Burns had been something of a scandalous character, prone to drink and overindulgent in sex. He had been arrested for digging up a body at a cemetery. Somehow he eluded jail time. He'd been known to carry handguns, though those few close to him claimed he was a very gentle creature. The realm of humanity saddened and angered him. They called him a genius, he called himself an explorer.

"He was the ultimate angst-ridden artist," Julie said with reverence.

"Don't burn any holes in your panties, Julie, this guys worse than married, he's dead."

"That's not certain."

"I know, but it's a nice thought," Kim snickered. "Oh, gotta go, my ride's here."

In a flutter of motion Kim was out the door. Julie was half-glad. She preferred the world when it was just she and Shemp and her own unchallenged thoughts. Outside the street was all hissing rainy traffic, the mindless bustle of human activity. She sat staring at the haunting paintings of Ryan Burns.

Though the subject matter was blatantly morbid, there was an evocative quality to the art that she found strangely infectious. The darkness of the blacks, the melancholy tones of grey, and the carefully strewn whites, tugged like gravity at her eyes. She could almost reach into the paintings and feel...

«« — »»

Boston was greyer than usual in the rain. Julie glimpsed her reflection as it fluttered ghost-like across drop-riddled puddles. She made it to the station then sat on the bus with her knapsack in her lap by an old man. She studied her co-passenger inconspicuously as the vehicle jiggled along, observing the deep dark of his wrinkles as if her eyes were a tongue tracing over them. The man seemed dazed. He stared ahead with fog-steeped eyes, mumbling occasionally. He drooled. Julie could almost feel the life trailing away from his shriveled body, as if the motion of the bus were leaving it behind in the street to run with the rain down into the Boston sewers. She felt an urgent fear for him, felt as if she should tell the bus driver to slow down so that this man's life energy could catch up.

Where did that energy go, Julie—like Ryan Burns—wondered. Where was Mommy? The question was like an ache. Burns had hunted for the answer, exploring the ruins of smashed cars, the scenes of suicides and murders. At the age of thirty he had vanished, and now Julie wondered if he had found the answer.

The magazine had quoted Burns' lover Susan Reed as saying that Burns believed he had discovered something important. Critics had long remarked on the uncanny tangible quality of his works, the measured precision of his brush strokes, yet these were more than smears of paint to Burns. They were the shadows of death. He claimed that his paint was a mixture of actual shadow and other unspecified substances—a transcendent concoction that made his pictures not so much true to life, as true to death. It was generally believed that Burns was insane and that he had committed suicide.

«« — »»

The Museum of Fine Arts was brooding brick in the afternoon cool. Julie's umber helmet of shortish hair jounced as she rushed up the stone steps. Inside the building was echoes and dignity, vast halls of paintings and stoic statues. She headed straight to the second floor, tapping a pamphlet impatiently against her thigh.

They were easy to spot, amidst all the colored works. The stark black and whites caught her as if she were a dust mote and inhaled her. Julie's sneakers squeaked on the waxy floor as she approached, the hum and flutter of internal organs playing havoc with her lunch.

There were two of them. The first showed a seagull lying on a beach, its body coated in thick glistening oil from a tanker spill. Its wings looked ragged, the feathers in disarray from struggling. The eye stared out in what appeared to be confusion and horror, the little bead brought disturbingly to life by Ryan Burn's talented hand. Poor thing, lying there in a glutinous pool of black shadow.

The other picture, entitled *Abrupt Stop* showed the front view of a wrecked car. The smashed headlights were like jagged skull sockets, the grill crushed and torn like a hideous black sneer. Julie leaned close as her eyes moved over the details. The shadows under the car seemed deep, as if they were not merely an area of pavement blocked from the sun's reach, but more like a hole.

Julie could all but smell the scene, the smoking fumes of gasoline, the heavy nasal weight of spilled oil, the strange organic-metallic blend of carnage. She could almost hear the thing as well, as if the dark paint was a liquid containing the sounds of the accident, pouring into her ears, each detail preserved in horrific over-amplification. A shrill shriek of brakes, the terrible slap of impact, protracted screams fading into a gurgling gel, the sounds of organs ripping wetly and glass bits skipping crisply down the road.

Julie was so absorbed that she was not aware of anyone else around her. She found her hand rising and reaching, like an object dropped and falling, as it came within inches of the deep black paint...

"Miss?"

The voice was an ice pick jabbing into her spine. Julie flinched and spun. A middle-aged man in a grey suit stood above her, looking down.

"We'd prefer that people wouldn't touch the paintings."

Julie flushed. "Oh, right. Sorry."

She looked down at the floor and shuffled quickly away, sneakers scuffing. She did not look back at the paintings. She had seen enough.

«« — »»

Toward the end of October most of the trees had spent their leaves. Maples stood as frayed pillars supporting the drooping roof of clouds. Julie sat in a puddle of rasping rust-colored discards with an art pad leaning on her thighs and a stick of charcoal poised. Her back was up against one of the old slate gravestones, an impassive winged face, and the words *memento mori* looking down over her shoulder.

The cemetery was a sprawling quiet place, so Julie deemed it safe to let Shemp wander without his leash. She would hear if any cars were about; besides, she was on a hill and Shemp could not easily stray from sight. The little fellow had perked up at being out in the open, trotting along on the paths with his ears jiggling. Occasionally Julie had to urge him to sit and rest, for his eagerness to explore was greater than his physical strength. He would sit reluctantly, panting, anxious to up and go. Julie feared he would suffer heart failure and wondered if bringing him was such a good idea.

She frowned at the sketch. It seemed weak. The graves were too small and the sky was too light. She took her charcoal and smudged it back and forth over the existing clouds, then used the side of her finger to blend it in. Yes, that was better.

It had been several weeks since she had given much thought to Ryan Burns. She had been busy with school, and the loss of Roger had drained much of her ability to feel inspired about anything. She had, however, tracked down as many articles as she could on the artist, and was presently waiting for a back issue of a publication which had done an interview with him. That would prove interesting.

Julie shifted her weight, her nest of leaves hissing. She looked up from her picture, absently scanning the surroundings for Shemp. He was nowhere in sight.

"Shemp? Here, boy!"

Grass and stones. Stillness.

"Shemp! Come on!"

Julie tossed her pad aside and stood up; the grey emanation of her shadow stretched away, down the hill. Her heart began to canter as she jogged down the slope, looking from side to side.

"Damn it! Shemp! Here, boy!"

The woman moved more quickly as adrenaline propelled her legs. Gravestones flashed past on either side, trimmed hedges blurred. Leaves crunched and danced as the intruder moved through their heaped pools.

"Please, God…"

A great crash of thunder in Julie's chest. There lay Shemp behind an old slab, flat on his side.

"Shemp!"

She knelt and put a hand on his chest. He was panting hard as he turned a cataract eye to take in the blur of his friend. Julie lifted him gently; Shemp nestled his snout against the familiar warmth of her neck.

《《——》》

The dream was more a product of Julie's renewed interest in Ryan Burns than an instigator of it. Although she did not realize it at first, her pursuit of information on Burns intensified as the dog grew sicker. It was as if watching Shemp draining away urged her desperately to find out where he was draining to. Like that old man that time on the bus. If the soul did exist, where did it go? The answer seemed to be in Burns' paintings.

In the dream the artist appeared at the foot of the bed, sliding out of the darkness, half his face in shadow, like in his self-portrait. Julie sat up and cast aside her covers, crawled to the edge of the mattress and reached out. She went to touch the shaded half of his face but her hand felt only darkness, not flesh, and her arm sank in to the elbow before her screams jarred her awake.

The next three days were busy. On the first she took Shemp back to the vet. Heart congestion, the doctor told her, a common condition for a dog that age. His kidneys were going too, and he was almost completely blind, as well as losing his hearing. The vet suggested that she put him to sleep.

The following day Julie did something she had wanted to do, but felt awkward about—she went to see Susan Reed. The college student had tracked down the woman's phone number and address and called ahead, claiming that she was doing a paper on Burns for school. Reed was reluctant at first, but then agreed to talk.

«« — »»

Reed and the apartment she lived in were disheveled. The woman was in her mid-thirties, though she looked older. She had frenetic brown hair and watery green eyes. Julie was perceptive enough to realize that the woman was an alcoholic, as well as a chain-smoker. Reed wore baggy clothing, so the condition of her body remained ambiguous. The most notable thing about her appearance was the stump where her left hand had once been.

Julie was nervous, but managed to give her questions in measured doses. She broke the ice with technical questions about Burns' style and schooling before probing into his personal past. Curiously though, Reed could offer little in that area that the articles had not covered. Burns had never revealed much about his past to the woman.

They ended up talking for several hours. Reed became more talkative the more she drank. Julie's inhibition weakened, too. She was thrilled when Reed showed her several of the originals she still had (she guiltily admitted to selling some in order to keep from being evicted). A couple of these depicted murder victims sprawled outside a Boston bar and another showed a deer with its tongue hanging out and a dark flower of blood where a hunter's bullet had violated. Julie, at last, had her chance to touch the paint itself, but, disappointingly, it felt like regular dried oil.

It seemed an appropriate time to spring the important questions.

"Miss Reed, what can you tell me about Ryan's alleged shadow paint?"

Reed swayed in her seat and chuckled darkly. She rubbed absently at the side of her nose with her stump.

"He called it his secret recipe. He mixed a special liquid up, then went to the scenes of these crashes and deaths, and poured some of the mixture into the shadows there. It would absorb some of the shadows and turn black. See, he felt that the shadows at these places were imprinted with a residue, that some sort of astral veil was impacted by these, these traumas and horrors. The shadows sort of changed and became a murky barrier between our world and, well, whatever. The paint, if it was comprised of actual shadow, would capture that. You know what I mean?"

Julie didn't know what to say.

Reed drew at her cigarette, hissed out a stream, and said, "But, the paintings were just his way of showing things, and venting things. No one knows about his real work."

"What was that?"

"He wanted to know the nature of things…life and death."

Julie leaned forward. "Did he kill himself, Miss Reed?"

The woman's eyes had a distant look for a long moment. She rubbed at the end of her stump with her intact hand. "I don't really know. He, he went into the shadows."

"How? Did he paint a doorway or something?"

Reed emptied her glass of brandy. "No, no. Not a painting, the paint."

Julie sat back in her chair and hugged her arms about herself. "Do you believe that?"

"You're fucking right I do—my hand went with him."

«« — »»

The next day, after her classes, Julie stole into the biology department at the college. She had successfully coaxed the secret paint recipe out of Susan Reed, and now carried the scrawled instructions in her coat pocket. She slipped unnoticed into the anatomy museum where full human skeletons stood like grinning sentinels watching over the varied bottles containing human body parts.

It had been no accident that one of Ryan Burns' close friends had been a pathologist. The man had provided Burns with the human organs needed to mix his special concoction. Julie managed to put her guilt aside as she slipped bottles into her knapsack. A formaldehyde-preserved heart and brain.

Afternoon was draining away when Julie arrived at the cemetery. The monuments were reaching across the autumn grass with protracted shadows. She had filled a jar with the substance, which included portions of liquefied brain matter and heart tissue, as well as water and a drop of blood and ingredients common to conventional oil paint. She made her way to her mother's grave, bent down, and stole some of the darkness that trailed like a plank from its base.

«« — »»

"I'll see ya Monday," Kim said. Her boyfriend was outside honking his car horn.

Julie glanced up from her notebook. "Oh. Okay. Bye."

The door slammed. Julie waited until she heard them drive away before taking out the jar. She stared in at the opaque substance…darker than ink, darker than anything she had ever seen. She set a small potted plant on the coffee table, unscrewed the top of the jar, and carefully poured a little out into the soil. The stems of the plant slipped quickly into the substance, then the leaves. It only took a second. The plant was gone and Julie found herself staring into the bottomless pit of the flowerpot.

«« — »»

Dawn was beginning to squeeze up over the eastern edge of the world when Julie was awakened by the coughing. She felt Shemp crawl out from the protective barricade of her fetal position and push free of the blankets. He paced around the bed a few times, then clumsily jumped down onto the floor.

"Shemp?"

Julie flicked on the light. Shemp was sprawled on his side in front of the door wheezing. The woman sprang from the bed and bent over him. She pressed her face to his side. His little heart was straining.

The vet! Call the vet!

"Please, Shemp, don't leave me, please!"

She knew what the vet would say. No. Shemp was not going to spend his last seconds of life on a cold steel table with a stranger poking a needle into him. She knew what she had to do.

Julie threw on a robe, and after placing Shemp on the bed, rushed into the bathroom and began filling the tub. She took the jar of black paint out of her closet and set it on the toilet cover.

Shemp seemed to be in a coma. Julie held him, rocking him, whispering, "I love you, I love you."

She looked around the room and everything seemed flat. At that moment, nothing in the world spoke to her, nothing meant anything. All she had was Shemp, but Shemp was draining away.

"Let's go," she said in a hush.

The tub was half full. She lay the dog on a towel and proceeded to pour the paint into the warm water. There was no steam, no magical flash or mad professor's laboratory gurgling—the water simply turned black.

Julie was resigned now. She had stopped crying. Gently she lifted Shemp, kissed him on the head and released him into the tub. There were no signs of drowning, no splashing or bubbling…he was gone.

The young woman removed her robe and stood naked, looking into the substance. She held the lip of the tub and raised one leg up and over; the other followed, into the black. She lowered her hips down, felt the warm wetness as it rose across her lower belly, accepted her navel, continued. Then she lost her nerve.

"Oh, God!" Panic! What was she doing? She could no longer feel her legs!

"Help!" Julie pushed down on the sides of the tub and yanked herself back. The water rippled in agitation. She managed to toss herself over the side. Thump. Julie looked down toward her legs, but there was only floor. She reached down—her body ended just inches below the sternum!

"No! No! Oh, Christ!" Frantic arms pulled the torso out into the living room. She was hysterical, tears streaming, the neat bloodless stump of her waist dragging.

She made it to the phone, grasped the cord and pulled it off the table.

"Nine one one, nine, one one…"

She poked at the buttons, but they were blurred by her tears.

A recorded voice came on… "We're sorry; your call cannot be complete—"

"Damn it!" Julie threw the phone. A lamp shattered and dial tone droned.

Julie struggled her way to the door and reached for the knob. It opened.

"Help! Somebody help me! Call the police! Half my body's gone!"

She dragged herself along the dirty old hall carpet.

Someone downstairs yelled, "Hey—shut the fuck up, or I'll call the cops!"

"Help! Get help, please!"

She used the banister rungs on the landing like a horizontal ladder and tugged herself to the top of the stairs. She heard the door of the apartment below slam shut.

"No, don't go, I—"

Julie tried to climb down the stairs and fell. She rolled, thumping, a pale torso with arms flailing. Pain. She lay at the bottom gasping, her ribs burning. Trembling, and on the brink of passing out, Julie got the front door open and crawled outside. She tumbled down several more steps, across the sidewalk and into the street.

"Somebody please help me!"

The sun was just beginning to scale the horizon of sleeping grey buildings. A crisp copper glow.

Julie looked like an animal, up on her elbows, laboring to get back to the sidewalk. The driver of the car, who barely noticed her until the impact, thought she was a white dog.

Thud! The torso was flung into the gutter. The car screeched to a stop and the driver rushed out. He saw half of a naked woman lying there and fell to his knees, vomiting.

Julie moaned. She tasted blood, felt warm trickling on her face. Her organs—what was left of them—were in spasm. She rolled over onto her chest, her hands shaking as they wrapped around the rusty bars of a sewer grate. She peered down into the glistening black below.

Sirens. A police car pulled up, blue lights pulsing. The sun flashed as it cleared the distant rooftops and the car, blocking the morning beams, cast shadow over the abbreviated naked woman.

Julie felt the cool dark as it poured across her back. She clung to the sewer grid and pressed her face between the bars as her life drained away. At first she thought that her face had gone numb, for she could no longer feel the grid. Then, she felt the welcoming warmth of Shemp's familiar tongue as he swabbed the tears from her cheeks.

OVER THE DARKENING FIELDS

Over the darkening fields, the east is an empty blue, above the shadow trees, by the cemetery of my youth. The rustling breeze, the cooling air, the smell of the field, all as if something is waking, as the day is lured to its sleep. Pass the rusted crown of the moon to the darker hours, above the fields and the small, helpless town.

Autumn brings me here, to the farm fields by the meandering graveyard, familiar New England hills fading. The light wanes; the sky is flat blue and vast, the fields dusky with shadow which seems to rise from below. The moon is a shard of ghostly crockery, impassive and patient, through woven trees.

Crickets brave the quiet where crows made their bold and hungry noise and my feet whisper in dry leaves. The sky has nothing to say, its summer rumbles quenched and past. Only the moon speaks, its pallor a song of watery light. The distant hiss of cars seems small within that quiet, under the great sky.

The west finishes with its copper, hangs there over the houses, paints them all black, even as they stir inside. Families home from school and work and bustling tasks, safe in the light of televisions and the aroma of their meals. Inside, they are oblivious to the size and secrets of the sky.

The chill has reached beneath my clothes, peered into my bones. Faint stars open like infant eyes and I count them. Soon there will be patterns, older than the houses that stand beyond the cemetery, to the west. Houses like cardboard. Tall grass shivers in the harvested field.

I raise my hands to the sky, raise my hands like pale spiders, tracing the lay of the stars. I repeat the motions, carefully. I summon the east— I cannot hear the sitcoms, I cannot hear the clinking of forks on dinner plates, I cannot hear the commercials, the music, the laughter, the lies from the houses. I cannot hear my heart. I only hear the east and it is silent.

I turn to the west, see a large house beyond the stone pillars of the burial grounds. It is hunkered in the dimness, but the windows are warm with light and humans move past the shades, drawn against me and the night. I hold my hands out and the east moves through me, from over the field, a darkness in the darkness, little more than a breeze reaching down to the house.

There is no panic, no screaming, there is nothing really, nothing left of the blind hulking house —it is simply gone.

The crickets pause, the moonlight makes a ghost of the field, the sky floats over the town and I swing my arms, conducting a symphony of stars. There is only shadow and grass where the big house stood. Another vanishes and another and more after that. One by one the houses are gone and the town, as I once knew it, looks more and more like a field, under the darkening sky.

HINDENBURG KISS

New York, 1936

It was an awful day to fall in love, if that was indeed what happened. One would think that after thirty-five years upon this spinning rock, the sensation would announce itself in a straightforward manner. I thought I'd known it as a younger man, and younger than that—a dizzy fool for this girl or that, over-dramatic, brazen and terrified. I'd known too well the desperate, giddy laughter that stung beneath the skin. How many one true loves had there been? How many times had my heart been smashed to bits, only to reassemble? No, it was an awful day to fall in love, because it was the last thing I expected.

Snow in New York City. It seemed pretty enough, but didn't it make the buildings look grey, the tall ones shorter, their upper floors erased. There were carolers and slush and the smell of idling cars as I walked out of the stoic embassy in front of my employer's wife.

"It's snowing!" Alice said, with a girl's beaming discovery. Two simple words and my heart stood up in my chest. It wasn't the words, so much as her sea-colored eyes, I tend to think now. I was no stranger to her eyes, mind you, nor the rest of her face. She was pretty enough, with mannered and pleasantly aging features, her hair brushed with September frost. But, it was the surprise—the sudden girl peeking out like a blossom from the diplomatic mask, the eyes free, for that one snowy moment.

I opened the door of the car by the curb and she ducked back into her shiny black world.

«« —»»

I began to watch for the girl after that. I knew she was there, a flower pressed between secret pages, dormant and subdued. I fancied myself a detective of sorts, looking for evidence of her existence. I listened hard to her laughter, but there was no girl to be heard. Alice's laughter was measured and appropriate, a dignitary's device, like a handshake, or perfect clothes. Perhaps I had erred in looking for the obvious.

Months passed and I watched, the image of her eyes stored away.

I was secretary to the British ambassador, at best an echo, at my worst inconsequential. I was a "yes' in a suit and tie, stiff as a chess piece, faithful as a fool. Partly ambitious, partly comfortable, it was my profession to hover. Over time, I came to realize that Alice and I were much the same in that respect.

Never one for epiphany, it came to me over time…I had been witnessing the girl all along.

«« —»»

The rain was grey as if New York were melting and the wind smelled of the river. It was the three of us, that raw afternoon, our umbrellas speaking their hollow rain language as we rushed for the car.

Desmond was talking; he was always talking, as if the world were always listening. Didn't much matter—it was the only voice he ever really heard. His voice saying whatever and mine saying "yes." Alice saying what was expected and more and more, nothing at all.

Something kicked out from under Alice's step and she stopped to see what it was. The small empty shoe of a doll, abandoned on the wet sidewalk. She stopped, as I said, stopped and turned and stared down at the thing, her umbrella off guard so that rain fell in her face like tears—all the rain in New York like her tears. She looked heartbroken—for the lonely toy, for the child that lost it. It was the face of the girl, the face of a sad little girl. She had been there all along.

"Coming?" Desmond whirled.

Alice looked over at me, saw the pain and smiled, ever so slightly, recognizing the sad little boy.

《《—》》

I lit her cigarette after dinner, my hands cupped around her hand, but not touching, the brief warm light on both our fingers. She sat back holding her drink, gazing into it as if dreaming a lost golden summer. Desmond was going on about something, chuckling sourly. I wondered if she hated his laugh as much as I did—his laugh like a jabbing knife of shale.

"Isn't that right, dear?"

Alice was lost in her glass, the reflection on her cheek like forgotten sunlight.

"*Alice?*"

"Yes, dear," Alice said, "of course."

There was a vase of cut flowers on the table, the stems stuffed tightly into the glass. Alice pulled one free and held it to her face, inhaling, the pink petals brushing her lips. I watched her mouth after that, drawn to the songs that slumbered, the warmth in its mask of lipstick, the words of love in an unborn language of kisses. Ahh, for one kiss, one sad, soft kiss.

《《—》》

New Jersey 1937

She is always soft in my memories, now, her hair going silver, like moonlight, the quiet white of her skin, the Atlantic-colored eyes. She whispers past in the rain when the busy day permits, always an ache away. The kiss itself is questionable, a blur. I must tell you of the kiss.

The three of us had driven down to the Lakehurst Naval Air Station in New Jersey to see the German Airship Hindenburg. Alice wanted so badly to see it; while terrified of heights, she was fascinated by the thought of flying.

Out with the great hangars and the wide May fields, we waited with the rest of the civilian spectators and ninety or so members of the Navy personnel. The sky was bigger than any sky, and the storm clouds let the sun through briefly.

Desmond checked his watch and grumbled about how the ship was late.

"Look!" Alice pointed and I saw the girl press up behind her face. I wanted to hold her just then—one kiss!

The zeppelin looked like an almond at first as it floated in from the Southwest. The almond grew to the size of a whale and the sun winked as if the windows were pennies before the rain returned, falling lightly.

The crowd was full of murmurs as the behemoth slowed. We could hear the mighty diesel engines reversing when it approached a massive docking mast.

Alice turned to me and said, "It's beautiful."

"Beautiful," I repeated.

A mooring rope dropped from the nose of the ship.

Alice's face was so close just then.

7:25 p.m. The Hindenburg burst—a great cloud of flame! From the upper rear fin to the fat middle, there was billowing fire. Seconds only and the airship was collapsing through the air, blazing, the brittle skeletal framework exposed, folding, falling. I can still hear the screaming, I can see the tiny people leaping out as it plummeted, but mostly, I see my shadow and Alice's shadow, sketched starkly by the burning craft. While we never touched, our shadows, in profile, distorted by the tumult of flames, rippled and shifted and for one brief moment, it looked as if they kissed.

THE WICKHAMPTON BLEEDING

The outbreak of what local lore refers to as the Wickhampton Bleeding, was first brought to my attention on July 7th, 1986. I was vacationing in Falmouth, MA when an unconscious man was dragged from the surf. The victim had been swimming while intoxicated. Myself and a retired nurse named Beth Richards attempted to revive the man, but he expired. In subsequent conversation, Mrs. Richards related a curious tale of a localized disease of which I had never heard.

Mrs. Richards offered a rudimentary version of the incident; seven people had been fatally afflicted in a British fishing village in the year of 1887. Intrigued by the peculiar particulars, I traveled to Wickhampton while visiting the United Kingdom. I pieced together as much information as I could, despite the reticent locals.

The first to be stricken was fifteen-year-old Patsy Lewis who became feverish and dizzy following a walk on the beach where she had found a weathered wooden breast, presumably from a broken figurehead (there had been a particularly violent storm the previous night). The girl's condition worsened steadily over the next few days. The local doctor, Harris Stockdale, observed bleeding ulcers in the patient's throat. She suffered delusions. She was convinced that it was raining sheep teeth and that the house was filled with a strange shrill whistling. Four days after the initial symptoms appeared, Patsy succumbed, violently hemorrhaging from the throat. In his journals, Dr. Stockdale reported that the blood on the girl's blankets made a great stain that resembled a beautiful woman's face.

Within days Patsy's parents and the doctor fell ill and experienced a similar series of symptoms, ultimately perishing as the girl had. Bizarre as it seems, in each case, and in the other three to eventually die from the malady, the blood that escaped from the patients appeared to shape that same female face. One victim coughed out a quantity of blood onto the ceiling, others dripped on the floors or in chamber pots —in each case that same face seemed to manifest itself, each portrayal more detailed and distinct than that which preceded it. None could identify the woman in the strange portraits.

Following the death of the seventh patient, a sheep farmer named Newberry, the Wickhampton Bleeding came to an abrupt stop. Some claim that it ceased when someone tossed the wooden breast that the Lewis girl had found into a fireplace, destroying the thing. Others superstitiously relate the Bleeding to a mysterious wreck ten years before. Apparently a vessel broke up in a storm and littered the beach with several drowned bodies, one a beautiful woman in chains. It was never discovered who the people were or where they had come from. I could coerce little more than what I have noted here, yet it was my impression that there was more to the tale than I was allowed access to.

One final note on the mysterious wreck at Wickhampton; a wooden figurehead washed up along with the bodies. The carving was said to be a ghastly thing, a combination of a woman and a serpent. It was thrown back into the sea following the unexplainable deaths of several villagers, but no one in Wickhampton wanted to talk about that.

PART

—

TWO

A MISHAP AND ITS AFTERMATH

It is often the case that the most fantastic episodes go unnoticed by history, unrecognized by science and entirely lost from all manner of records, but perhaps for the obscure and seldom-shared memory of this or that individual. The following is just such a specimen.

The key event took place in the midst of a damp September in the year of 1883. As if it were not cruel enough that Mrs. Emma Lindon had recently been widowed, she set about her business unaware in the drizzle, while fate or something worse hunched over its grim plans, waiting.

Common to the hour in that segment of London, there was a great deal of activity, all manner of comings and goings—a rainy blur of motion and noise. Accompanied by her young daughter Mary—a mere three years of age—she paid visit to the baker and the hat shop. She towed the girl by the hand along the busy street and yielded when the window of the toy shop—an irresistible clutter of bright, colorful enchantments—took control of Mary's attention.

Keenly sympathetic to the rawness of her offspring's loss, she had found herself as late attempting to bandage the tot with distractions. Mary's chest of toys, following the death of her father, was over-flowing. So in they went.

Mary was specific for her age and took a great deal of time in choosing the right thing. Today it was a bright striped ball the size of a coconut. Mrs. Lindon paid from her purse and they returned to the street, the child clutching her ball as if it were a source of heat.

Chaise and driver waited nearby beneath a street lamp just ahead of a larger stationary carriage. Buggies and carts of produce wheeled across the slick cobblestones, and those travelers on foot moved briskly to counter the chill. There was such an accumulation of noise, that the young Mrs. Lindon heard not the thump of a ball when she stopped to indulge herself in a wistful stare. She observed a handsome couple kissing beneath a shared umbrella across the way, and scarcely noticed that Mary's small hand had slipped from her own.

Mary pursued her new round treasure as it bounced into the gutter and came to a rest in a puddle beneath the larger of the carriages. She bent to retrieve it, pressing up against the spokes of the vehicle's rear wheel.

Unaware, the driver of the tall carriage snapped his whip at his team and the vehicle lurched forward. There was not so much as a cry from the girl, for the spokes had her by the neck and she spun grotesquely with their motion as if a doll.

Alerted by the shouts of others, Mrs. Lindon looked hopelessly upon the scene and, dropping her hatbox and the box of pastries, ran screeching. There was such a commotion from onlookers that the driver brought his carriage to a halt, but by then the damage was done and the child lay snared, beyond repair. Mrs. Lindon wailed piteously above the ruin.

«« —»»

The young widow occupied an important-looking brick house from the time of the last George. For all the grandeur of the furnishings and the spaciousness of the rooms, it was a stoic climate minus music and laughter, and the servants moved stealthily in deference to their mistress' state.

As one may well assume, Emma proved distraught. Her driver had lifted Mary into their chaise and brought her to the residence where she was laid out in a parlor. The doctor was summoned as was Harry, her brother, a solicitor.

Harry determined to tend all necessary arrangements but there was no relief to be had for his sibling. She sat by the pale wreckage, holding a cool hand, sobbing. The doctor, whose skills were superfluous under the circumstances, delivered his condolences and excused himself.

The hour grew late and Harry proposed that he remain for the night, but Mrs. Lindon refused him. Solitude was her only desire, and she spoke harshly when a servant attempted to sponge spots of blood from the carpet at the doorway.

Promising to return in the morning, Harry bid farewell and returned to the rain. Mrs. Lindon was left to her purpose and gathered things appropriate to the task at hand, fetching knives from the kitchen and her sewing implements as well.

Exhibiting an admirable precision, Emma set about opening the body of her child. She had piled the tables with candles and burned the lamps high; she hunched like a surgeon until the meticulous work was complete. Afterward she sewed the remains shut and woke her servants to dig in the garden.

«« — »»

First light was upon the grand brick house when Harry, true to his promise, arrived by chaise. He banged with the knocker until the door was opened to some small degree and the wearied face of a house-keeper peeked out.

Upon orders from her mistress, the woman informed Harry that no company was to be admitted. Harry balked, as you might well imagine, but his insistence got him no farther than the threshold. At length the man accepted defeat and, flustered, departed.

At least as stubborn as his bereaved sister, Harry made every conceivable attempt to win audience with her, to no avail. His letters went unanswered and his presence at the door was customarily met by the fatigued face of the servant. The missus was seeing no one, he was told.

It was soon discovered that Harry's isolation was not exclusive—it would appear that each of Emma's friends had been denied contact as well. Indeed, the widow Lindon might have fallen off the Earth, so far as anyone outside of that brick monolith was concerned.

«« — »»

Winter came to the city, and a note of intrigue was interjected into Harry's day when a certain woman called upon his offices. Clementina Haslem, Emma's closest and dearest friend, informed the solicitor that she had witnessed no small amount of activity coming about at Emma's fortress. Her own eyes had witnessed a number of masons and a considerable quantity of bricks gaining entrance to the aforementioned structure. The man thanked his visitor and investigated to the best of his abilities, but nothing further was gained.

When next Mrs. Haslem paid visit to Harry's firm, she was in a much disquieted state. It was the spring of 1884 and she had been about some business in town when she saw—or thought she saw—Emma Lindon.

Harry sat his guest down and soothed her with tea. Clementina recounted her experience, trembling so that her cup and saucer rattled. She had been going about her ordinary day, as mentioned, when she became aware of the figure of a woman some distance away. This figure seemed familiar, though the bonnet on her head and the shadows of the buildings meant to obscure her. Still, an impression had been made and she took up pursuit.

Having paused to gaze into the window of a toy shop, the woman—who appeared to be holding a baby in her arms—inadvertently afforded Clementina the opportunity to shorten the distance between them.

It was about this time that the keen crying of a babe was heard. It was an especially shrill sound, almost painful to the ears, and it appeared that Clementina was not alone in marking it, for passersby gawked at or steered around the young mother, passing in the gutter, grimacing.

When only a short length separated the two women, and Clementina saw the other's face more clearly, she called out. Emma—for it was in fact Harry's sister—regarded her old friend with a look of horror and promptly spun in an attempt to flee. The appearance of a boxy gent worked favorably for Clementina, for Emma collided with the man and her escape was delayed. Clementina caught her by the arm, cringing at the volume of the baby's wailing. Denied her evasion, Emma stared mute and pale at her old confidant.

At this point in the story, Harry, captive to his own agitation, interrupted, noting that he had possessed no knowledge of the fact that his sister had been with child, if indeed the screeching babe were her own.

Clementina shared his ignorance on the matter, and became entirely discomposed when she recounted what next transpired.

Having just encountered her friend after a lengthy separation, Clementina had inquired of the woman's state and, inspecting the deafening bundle, sought some explanation as to its history. But no response whatsoever was returned. Emma only gaped, her features stamped with alarm which was seen to worsen when Clementina reached to pull back the wrap from the child's face.

Here Harry's visitor took to sobbing and he consoled her, prompting gently, asking what then?

When the cloth was peeled back, there was no baby to be seen, for the bundle was occupied wholly by the moist brown slab of an organ, from which the cries emitted, despite the fact that there was no mouth to produce them. There were no features at all, merely a glistening dark mass.

Upon revealing the anomaly, Clementina fell in a faint and when she roused, both Emma and the swaddled object were not to be seen.

«« — »»

That very afternoon Harry called upon his sister's house. Once more he encountered the servant and was denied admittance. He raged at the woman and she hastened to bolt the door against him.

Harry paced on the walk, cursing, and then took note of a man he recognized as a neighbor of his sister. He swiftly introduced himself and fired questions at the poor fellow. The gentleman was agreeable, and offered as much as he knew.

According to this Mr. Turnbridge, Emma had become a reclusive creature following the tragic mishap, which had stolen the life of young Mary. Sometime later, though, the sound of an infant's bawling was heard by those in the immediate vicinity of the Lindon residence. Even from the street he was acutely aware of the wails, for they pierced the building's brick walls as if they were little more than muslin. The cries only stopped once the masons had finished up their work at the place.

The man further explained that his wife had, as late, seen Emma in the street carrying her loud child. Had Mrs. Turnbridge actually seen the child in close proximity? She had not.

Harry thanked the man and turned back to the house of his sister, determined to gain entry.

«« — »»

Servants rushed to the parlor when they heard the smashing of the window. There they found Harry standing in a glinting puddle of glass. He snarled at them and urged them away, brandishing his umbrella as if a saber, and proceeded to stomp through the lower floor of the house, investigating each room.

The crying of a baby was not to be heard and there was no trace of his sister. Harry pounded up the stairs. In the upper hallway he encountered the housekeeper—she was yanking at a chord which presumably signaled a bell on the other side of a great metal door fastened to a newly constructed wall of brick.

Harry shoved the servant out of his way and when the door cracked open, he was nearly repelled by the deafening cries from within. Emma peered out and gasped; Harry pushed her and the door aside, marching into the room.

He found himself in a windowless chamber of brick, a curious cross between a prison cell and a nursery. He went directly to the bed and tore back the curtains.

Dear God, he breathed, upon viewing the occupant.

At first glance he took it to be a roasted swan, squirming there on the bed, but the thing was not a bird. It was plump and damp and only loosely shaped but for the tiny pink arms and legs poking out. The source of its cries was not a mouth—they seemed to radiate from every part of it.

It's Mary, Emma wept, covering her mouth with her hand.

Harry stood and stared, despite the noise. The mass on the bed wriggled pitifully, the miniature legs kicking. The fingers of one little hand groped blindly at the colorful coconut-sized ball that had been placed in the bed beside it.

Mary, Harry muttered.

«« — »»

Emma went on to tell her brother all. She told him how she opened her daughter's body and removed some intact bit and swaddled it, rocking it by the fire, whispering. She told him how it grew and cried and how she felt the love coming through in its heat.

144

The thing in the bed would continue to grow, tended by its mother and its uncle (their ears stuffed with candle wax). At length it took the form of a pale little girl and a lovely young woman after that.

While Mary was largely confined to her sound-dulling chamber, her life proved happy enough. She played and read and communicated through notes, for even in her adult years she was incapable of speech. Not to say that she made no sound, for the shrieking never ceased. Even when she was happy, which was the better part of the time, the cries cast out from her flesh, her limbs and torso and hair, as much from her mouth.

Mary died unexpectedly on her twentieth birthday. She passed away in her sleep, mercifully enough, and it was plain to those who saw her that there was a pleasant smile upon her lips. The cries, however, carried on as before, echoing out from the still figure on the bed.

Throughout the years, when Emma and Harry brought flowers to Mary's second grave, they would hear the shrill wailing seeping up through the soil, like a breeze rustling the grass.

THE NYSSA

I have spent months up in this room, clutching a feather pen, my inky fingers black as coal. The steps and voices of the family below are something from another world, seemingly separated by more than the conventional layering of floorboards and ceiling plaster. They might be ghosts mumbling about, echoing, dragging furniture. Or maybe I am the ghost.

It is a room in an old frame house in a town with more farm fields than men. The chamber is simply furnished, and the one window looks out to the barn. I spend most of my time here at the writing desk, unaware of the hours, oblivious to hunger and the need for sleep. I have a story to tell, after all.

I write into the late hours, hunched over the paper with a quill, scribbling until my hand aches and the candle burns low. Then I fall onto the bed and sleep. My mind unalterably returns to the same dream, as if to the hallways of a familiar maze. But, for all its familiarity, the story is different each time, if in small ways.

Sometimes the characters are transposed, the settings altered. The only constant is the ending, and each night the dream reminds me of that.

One night I dreamed that Emeline was standing in the rain outside a museum in a city. Usually the city is Boston, or London, and once even Dublin, but this night it was a city without a name, a maze all to itself. She was in the rain and it was dark, and she was waiting for me. But where was I?

She was patient enough, and that was true to life. The rain thumped like little heartbeats on the dark skin of her umbrella. Time, it seemed, had become a liquid. It streaked and dribbled and puddled and poured. The ash-colored city was saturated.

At length a carriage rattled up and a stout fellow came bounding out, splashing his way toward the museum steps. Clearly he was not me, though the dreams have proven liberal in interpreting my height and weight. Rain drummed on his bowler and hissed when it found his cigar.

Emeline stepped back to avoid collision. His head was down and he was dashing like a wild boar—a well dressed boar. Everything in the city was darkly dressed.

Suddenly they were face-to-face, he looking up into that angelic white visage, and she down into his, a great, folded, bloodless fruit.

"So," the man said, "this is how it feels to be a sponge!"

The dream captured Emeline's lyrical laughter to a T.

"Yes, I should say," the young woman replied.

The man paused on the step below her, which only served to accentuate his shortness. He puffed against the deluge, but his cigar smoke was no match for the rain—its ghostly composition fragmented posthaste.

"Waiting for someone, I see?"

"Drowning for someone is more like it," was Emeline's ironic attempt.

The man barked out a laugh. "Making someone wait on such a night as this is a crime against punctuality."

Emeline almost looked apologetic, as if she might come up with some excuse on my behalf. The rain had found its way past her umbrella and her full black skirt was damp and sagging. She shifted her weight on wet shoes and glanced up and down the street, huffing.

"Well," the man said, climbing up a step, "I'm certain this person you're waiting for will understand if you take cover inside…"

Emeline smiled, flustered. "Why, yes. I'm sure you're right."

She waited for him to lead the way, which he did. The man passed her and trudged up the steps to the double doors of the grey stone building. It was a tall medieval thing; one would have expected the doors to creak more than they did.

Inside it was quiet until their feet scuffed on the flags. Or were those petrified puddles? It was dim, of course, as the entry to such a museum ought to be. They were standing in an arched foyer; more stairs climbed opposite the doors and led into a spacious lobby that the dream had dressed in dusky marble. The other visitors, few and shadowy, shuffled about in there.

"That's better, isn't it?" the little man asked with a grin.

"Much better, thank you, Mr..."

"Slumberton." He took her hand as if it were the hand of a queen and swept off his drippy bowler.

In prior renditions of this dream his name had been Skiffbatten, Stunthistle, and Sourbarrow.

"Emeline Westbracken," Emeline said with a shy smile.

"How lovely." The horrible little cigar, which moved like an auxiliary tongue, shifted to the opposite side of the man's scrunched face. He released her hand, bowed, and was off up the stairs. He called back as he scooted into the great hall. "I do hope your young man shows soon."

At this point the dream came to a stall. Emeline stood there in the foyer for the longest time, as if she were one of the displays. Even the drops on her folded umbrella hung in place, like rivets. Animation returned after a spell.

The doors rushed open and a young man blew in. He was more cloak than man, actually, and he moved straight past Emeline as if he didn't even see her. He vanished up the stairs, into the museum proper.

Emeline looked expectantly at the doors, hoping that someone else might come through, but this did not happen. Never had I seen such distress on her face; the dream alone afforded me this intimacy. She had likely made an effort to constrain such displays in my corporeal presence. The dream followed her up the stairs.

The hall, as I said, was lofty and dark. There were sconces here and there, and tempting openings to labyrinthine wonders. While the grand chamber was better lit than the foyer, those few others standing about were anything but distinct. People were reduced to hints...a glint of a cufflink here, the whisking hem of a skirt there, winking beads of rain on a bowler. Pearls like an abacus smile, bow ties hovering moth-like, a shoe cutting through the dimness—a miniature shark.

Emeline took a cautious step. She'd have made a fine blind woman the way she tested the dark with her folded umbrella. Not one to plow into an open space, be it bright or dim, she stuck close to a wall and made her way toward the nearest doorway. The doorway had the shape of a keyhole.

The exhibit was entitled The Nyssa.

There were portholes in the wall—dull, but enticing, and behind each an item pertinent to the theme. Emeline approached these as she had the spider webs in a grandmother's garden, with trepidation, and hungry for the jolt of fear that a glimpse of the weaver promised.

The reflection of her own pale features floated up in the first window, but faded when she pressed her hands to the sides of her face. A model warship hovered in a darkness of undetermined proportions. It was a majestic vessel with sails the color of her undergarments, and miniature canons peeking from gunports.

Emeline sensed someone close behind her, someone eager to see this particular display, so she moved along to the next. The porthole, complete with smeared handprints, revealed a sailor's uniform ground to a non-color by the sea's teeth. It hung wrinkled against an almost-black painting of the Atlantic.

The next showed a long, horizontally strung strip of bandaging. It was frayed, and spotted with dull flowers of rust. Emeline felt her stomach tighten below her ribs, the weight of her wet dress dragging at her like an undertow.

Another porthole showed a rusty flaking canon ball like a fossilized cabbage, another offered a teacup cluttered with barnacles. Others displayed coins and corroded silverware, a spyglass and tangled lengths of rigging.

Some of the portholes contained photographic works, muffled behind watery glass. One of these held Emeline's attention longer than the rest. It was a view of the harbor—before grand sea captains' houses sprouted up to block the water—a view seen from the entry of the museum. Women had gathered there to watch the Nyssa sailing off on her final voyage. "The Widows' Steps," the spot came to be called.

Emeline had her face pressed to the final portal when she smelled cigar smoke. Sitting behind the glass was an empty wooden chair.

"A terrible thing," a man's voice said.

Emeline turned and looked down at the puffing, black-clad countenance of Mr. Slumberton.

"Yes," she managed weakly.

"It was the Captain's fault," the man said, further scrunching his deflated face, "…never should have tempted the shoals in a gale such as it was."

Emeline blinked and nodded numbly. "They say he was the only survivor," she said.

The man barked a bitter laugh. "If you care to call it that."

Slumberton reflected for a moment, sighed, and then offered his hand. "Well, young lady, it's been a pleasure making your acquaintance, but I must be about my business."

Emeline took his hand. She gave it more of a squeeze than she had earlier. The hand was soft and squished like a sponge in her grip—water dripped down through her gloved fingers.

Slumberton turned to the port hole and pried it open. He stuck his head in, then, over his shoulder, asked, "Would you mind giving me a shove?"

Emeline dropped her umbrella on the floor, and bent to push the bottom of the man's feet as he squirmed through the opening. The man grunted, coughed a bit, and cleared the rim. Inside his little black womb, he brushed himself off, then sat dutifully in the empty chair facing the porthole, and the exhibition room beyond.

Usually, at this point in the dream, Emeline or the sad little man, closed the hinged window. This time it was Emeline's turn. She swung the thing back into place and stepped back to read the brass plaque over the glass. Sometimes it read Captain Skiffbattten, or Captain Sourbarrow, or Captain Stunthistle. In this version of the dream it noted: Captain Slumberton.

The man gave a salute and Emeline shuffled away, back to the great hall, and down into the foyer, then out to the rainy steps that once afforded her a view of the harbor. There she stood, waiting, hoping that there were *two* survivors of the wrecked Nyssa.

And that is how the dream, that repetitive assemblage of subconscious speculation, always ends.

I wake from the dream and return to my little desk, and my story. It is a story of wounds and floatation, of buoyant scraps of hull and staring crewmates like bobbing dolls. A story of an island, and a kindly family that took me from the shore and gave me shelter in their home. A kindly family that assures me that a ship will come by someday, a ship to sail me home to Boston, or London, or Dublin, or wherever it is I come from.

JULIA'S FANCY

London, 1888

She was black and white, lying on her back in a dark street, blurring in the September rain. The dreary buildings had soaked up some of the puddle, their angles ill-defined so that their windows looked to be floating in grey mist. Rain continued to fall, each drop casting tiny circles on impact as if a small invisible kitten were dancing on the water, drumming on the newspaper that lay in the gutter.

Mrs. Wilson was oblivious, going on about something, some minor scandal concerning a mutual acquaintance, no doubt. I nodded as if listening and stole another glance at our feet where the newspaper lay drowning.

Isn't that absolutely horrid? Mrs. Wilson said.

Absolutely, I replied absently. It hardly would have been ladylike to stoop and stare at the paper, of course, so I inconspicuously cast my eyes down. Mrs. Wilson was starting to annoy me.

"Can you imagine such a thing?" she asked.

"Dreadful" I said, "horrible."

Dread and horror were unacceptable elements in our social circles. I caught myself staring at the drawing of the dead woman on the front page of the soggy paper. The words were amorphous little insects and the woman's body, and even the policeman standing over it, looked ghostly as the ink became one with the pigeon-colored puddle.

"And to think-" My friend blathered distractedly as we stood there in the rain, our expensive fashions safe beneath drumming umbrellas, the familiar affluence of the fine street all about us.

Mrs. Wilson actually gasped when the impulse to lift the paper finally won out. The soggy paper began to tear in my hand, portions sloughing off as I brought it higher. I had a closer look at the drawing, but by then the image was besmeared as if someone had dragged a squid over it.

"Julia!" Mrs. Wilson barked. "Good heavens—put that dirty thing down!"

She slapped my hand and the paper flopped free, onto the wet cobblestones.

"Now look what you've done to your nice new glove" the woman scolded parentally.

The fingers of one glove were indeed stained—my hand appeared black and white.

«« —»»

I think I missed the smell of my husband's pipe more than I missed the man. Certainly there were things about him that I did not miss in the slightest, such as being introduced as his *lovely young thing*. The servants made for better company, in all actuality, though I would never say as much in the company of Mrs. Wilson and the rest.

My brunch-mate and I had parted in the rain and I had hurried home. I removed my wet things and settled in the parlor, comfy in my robe, with tea and a fresh copy of *The Penny*. Wouldn't my Harry have balked at that—having such a sensationalistic excuse for journalism in his house? But he would not return from the West Indies for some months yet, and so I indulged, unjudged.

The fire spat and I read. I sipped tea and thought of blood and the color it must have turned in rain. I studied the drawn picture as carriages clattered outside the window.

Somehow I had managed not to hear of the previous murder, at Bucks Row, but then I never had much patience for the news. The killing was a beastly thing, as was this second Whitechapel incident. Imagine. It was as if the man responsible—and it must have been a man, after all—made a ghastly art of maiming.

I could not recall having ever stepped foot in the sad neighborhoods of the Tower Hamlets, where the killings took place—they were as intangible to me as deserts in Africa or jungles in South America, or the Himalayas.

Having read the paper repeatedly, I moved to the window and gazed upon rain-colored London.

《《—》》

Dressed darkly, as if in disguise, I secured a cab next morning. The driver gave me a curious look when I told him where I wished to go. The day was grey and cool and I had brought an umbrella, in case. The cab clattered past the Royal Exchange, crossed Bishops Gate and continued on up into London's eastern sector—Aldgate, Whitechapel.

It was an impoverished place that passed my window as I sat safe in the womb of the carriage. Later I would conjure it in ink-wash and charcoal, my renderings seemingly incomplete without the filthy stench. It was an alien world, to be sure. My breeding had even spared me knowledge of such squalor.

Wretched women huddled outside of a common house smoking clay pipes, small unwashed girls in rags sold blood-red paper flowers on the street, neglected buildings leaned and loomed like shadows casting shadows.

"Here we are, missis," the driver said when at last we came to a stop.

I dismounted into the cool, smoky air and looked upon the spot where the first woman had been found. Such a dismal place to die—that was my first thought. They had found her on her back by the gate of a stable, a warehouse nearby. I knelt and touched my hand to the paving stones where Mary Ann Nichols' black bonnet had been found.

The driver stood by his animal, bewildered. He was patient enough, I'll be bound, and waited as if to guard me whilst I captured the scene in my sketchbook.

It began to drizzle about the time I arrived back in my familiar well-to-do environment. I asked that the driver oblige me one further stop, as there was something I wished to purchase. My business at the shop wrapped up, I made hastily back to the cab, for it had begun to rain in earnest. The rain drummed on the hatbox.

«« —»»

I had become—uncharacteristically—something of a glutton for newspapers. I read them that evening before retiring, while sipping a bit of sherry. Sherry had always made me drowsy and before long I retired to my chamber.

I fell asleep in my clothes, atop the bedcovers, my new black straw bonnet on my head and my skirt and petticoats bunched up nearly to my waist, as Mary Nichols' had been.

«« —»»

Whitechapel seemed more at home in the nighttime, its slums ghostly in fog (which was more coal smoke than drizzle). For this excursion I had requested that the cab wait off on an adjoining street while I walked the damp alleys, the gaslights shimmering on wet cobblestones.

I stood in the gloomy little yard where Annie Chapman had been found, her corpse by the wooden fence, the throat cut. There was the very spot where she had lain and bled—a rough quilt of paving stones and drab earth.

Careful to ascertain that I was alone, I went about my preparations. I had brought a long wool scarf and a smallish bottle of water. I soaked the scarf with the water and then lay down on the pavement at the bottom of the steps that led into the tall lodging house. I pulled my skirts up high above my legs and draped the soggy scarf about my left shoulder so that it weighted upon me as Annie's removed intestines must have weighed on her.

I remained only moments it seemed, with the cool ground beneath me, and the clammy air against my legs. My body thrilled indecently and I muffled a cry with my wrist.

«« —»»

The Ripper was busy come month's end. Two in one night on 30th, September. I visited each scene the following day, hovering amidst the others, kindred in morbidity. They did not tremble as I, least not for the same reasons.

I returned in the night and was about to lay on the spot in Berner's Street, but a besotted couple came round and entirely spoiled the moment.

More successful was my stop at Catherine Eddowes' death scene, by a fence in Mitre Square. I must have lain there a good three minutes or more. I positioned myself in the very same fashion as the prostitute had lay, according to printed accounts…my legs opened just so, my bodice and jacket undone and my skirts bunched up on my chest. The black bonnet (inspired by the first victim) proved handy—Eddowes was found wearing one as well.

Once more I made use of the damp muffler and further, emptied water directly on my throat and down the length of my ribs and belly to the lower abdomen. I took great pleasure in the sensations—the liquid and the chill breezes pouring across my flesh. True, it sent me into raptures, but somehow, it wasn't quite enough.

《《—》》

I found myself brunching with Mrs. Wilson near the middle of November. It was an appropriate location for people of our class to be seen at, mind you, but I was entirely engrossed in the day's news, even though this or that important wife stopped by our table to spew platitudes. I must have merely grunted at them distractedly as I attempted to devour the paper (more so than my meal).

My companion, the impeccable Mrs. Wilson, was no less troubling than if a great black fly were buzzing about my head. Where was Jack when one needed him?

It sounded as if The Ripper had done his best job yet.

"Oh," Mrs. Wilson at last noticed the headline, "one less harlot in the city…pity," she said, caustically. Then it was straight back to matters of importance… "Would you believe what that Mrs. Adamson was wearing on her head?"

From what I was able to take from the paper, a woman had been all but butchered in a room off Dorset Street, Whitechapel. Not only had her throat been sliced, like the others, but organs had been removed, an arm practically severed, and the nose was missing, to say nothing of the fact that her legs were stripped of flesh from foot to thigh.

"Would you pass the cream, dear?" Mrs. Wilson said.

I responded, and in so doing knocked my butter knife into my lap. My companion must have thought that the smile was for her.

«« — »»

Being lost just added to the thrill. The cab had dropped me off in the gloom and mist of Dorset Street, from which I found Miller's Court, easy enough. Adjacent to that was the little room where Mary Kelly had been dismantled. There was nothing to see, but I pressed my cheek to her door before I set off wandering.

Midnight chimed dully in the haze and my shoes sounded sharply on the cobbles as I wandered the tight, damp streets. It felt as if my organs were humming a cacophony of strange little tunes against the strangling fist of my bodice. I'd have preferred the feel of mist whispering against my flesh, or the clammy kiss of rain-slicked pavement.

"Where are you?" I caught myself saying into the dark.

I was clacking along a length of lonely warehouses, on Brick Lane, I believe, when I heard steps that seemed more than simply an echo of my own. I turned to face the sound and stood still to determine if there were, indeed, another set of feet sounding on the street. There were.

An indistinct figure appeared down the way, moving steadily, if slowly, in my direction. My heart accelerated and I wondered how it would feel…the blade going in, I mean. That was, after all, what I desired.

It was a man, that much was clear, but the combination of haze and lamp glow made him a rather amorphous shape. I set forward to meet him, smiling strangely. When a matter of yards separated us, I opened my arms, as if to embrace a dear old friend and the man raised up his hand—he was holding something. All of a sudden I found myself blinded by the light of a constable's bull's-eye lantern. I recoiled.

"Sorry, Miss, didn't mean to startle you," the officer said.

I laughed that anxious laugh of mine, the one that flies out when my nerves are moving faster than my mind. "Not to worry," I managed, collecting myself.

"Would you be lost, then, Miss?" he asked.

"Actually no—I'm just about a stroll is all."

Clearly he recognized me for something other than a native, and cautioned me, following a quizzical look. "You'd best be on yer guard, then—that monster's still about."

"Yes, well, thank you. I shall proceed with the utmost caution."

Seemingly placated, the officer drifted off. I went about my directionless way, favoring the darker streets where a handful of whores still hovered and drunken men skulked and staggered.

Several of the women eyed me suspiciously, others seemed too full of drink, or too destitute of spirit to pay me any mind. At any rate, I moved off into the cover of shadows.

A young man with something of a furtive air caught my attention. He came out from a public house called the Britannia and turned to head up the street. There I stood, loitering like a working girl, incongruously attired in my dark finery. He looked an angry fellow, the type that might enjoy stuffing a blade into a woman's body, his eyes being so dark and all.

"Excuse me," I heard myself call as he passed. He wheeled impatiently, but seemed to soften at the sight of me. He came close to where I stood, at a gap between two cheerless buildings.

"Yes?" his voice had something of a darkness to it, pleasingly enough. He looked me up and down with a refreshing lack of subtlety.

I took him by the hands and pulled him deeper into the alley so that the gaslights could hardly see us. He grinned and there was an arousing touch of gin on his breath.

"Jack," I said, smiling. "Here…"

I worked my buttons hastily as the man looked on. I tugged the layers aside, presented my bosom. I pushed my skirts lower so that my belly showed, pale and soft as a scallop. Then I took his hand and placed a thin knife in it. His pleasant expression changed.

"*Here*," I repeated, trembling. I guided his hand with my own, pressing the icy tip of the knife into my navel.

The young man gasped and stepped back. "What? You're mad!"

He threw down the knife and ran clacking out onto the misty street.

"Jack!" I called.

I sagged back against the wall and covered my face in my hands.

"Jack," I muttered, "where are you, Jack?"

《《——》》

If there was anything that privilege had taught me, it was that *anything* could be purchased, providing one possessed the means. With this philosophy in mind, I returned to the East End the following night, about a new course of action.

Whitechapel Road offered something of a circus atmosphere come Saturday night. A varied abundance of goods and services were made available, there in the fetid air, in the sickly glow of naptha lights. Everything from toys and meat to furniture and secondhand boots could be purchased. There were music halls and waxworks. Quacks peddled miraculous cures outside of public houses (where more potent liquids dwelt).

The raggedy masses thronged about, sang in the taverns; a quantity of men squandered their meager earnings on drink and women, some of whom were in such a state of desperation that their favors could be had for old bread.

It was there in that dismal dream-like atmosphere, that I happened on a fellow who was more than willing to indulge my latest fancy. He was a gaunt creature by any measure, with a beard like Saint Nick and small eyes like a ferret.

He took me into a dark, stale-smelling hallway, past a shadowy, groaning tangle of limbs. His flat was up a steep little staircase.

His room was brightly lit with candles and a sheeted table awaited. I disrobed as he prepared his tools.

"Not to fear, Miss," the man said, rolling back his shirt sleeves, "I'm the best at what I do."

"Oh, I'm not afraid," I said.

I lay down on the table and the man stood over me. Something metal glinted in his hand and I winced at the initial penetration. He was meticulous and patient—he worked on me for hours as I lay in his bleak little room, savoring the pain.

At one point I craned my neck to observe and saw the dark streaks running the length of my torso. I sighed and my head rolled back. My eyes rolled back.

««—»»

The dawn was as grey as the good old city itself—the low sky like a porridge of pigeons and slate and smoke from the factories. The churches made their Sunday noise and all the good folk crowded into their pews, their sinful flesh safe under finery and the echo of ancient words.

Some weeks had passed since last I paid visit to Whitechapel and wasn't I a thing of beauty, standing unclothed before the long mirror?

Permanent streams of blood ran down from the dark wound-marks on my throat, and my belly was a realistic display of exposed organs, the runny intestines like a nest of eels. Tattooed blood wound down my thighs, like pretty Christmas ribbons, pressed into the flesh.

I was a walking masterpiece—the tattoo artist had said as much, so pleased was he with his own workmanship. I had to admit he was right on that score. Still, I found myself not entirely satisfied.

There remain several weeks before my husband arrives back from overseas, and one may wonder what *he* will think of my embellishments. Not to be concerned. Tonight I return to look for my Jack. Surely I'll find him before Harry returns, either that or Jack will find *me*.

PART
—
THREE

THE CINNAMON MASK

ONE

It was a twenty-minute ride from the grey civility of Franklin Square Station to the seemingly abandoned streets of The Stain, where industry had once boasted and banged. The Great Fire had emptied and blackened the breweries crowded by the stagnant North River, and textile mills presented brick husks, their echoing bellies full of pigeons and leaves. Impressive in death, they were a monument to vanished prosperity.

Mr. Butterhill ducked out of his coach and opened his umbrella against the soggy day. An agent of The Crown, he stood out from the occasional regular, his suit being a fine dark thing and his full-head mask of better quality than the locals could afford. From the neck up he was a short-haired mammal with a blunt snout, the lightweight, finely crafted wood rubbed to a soft berry-scented sheen.

"I'm looking for the bookshop," he told a rag of a man in the street.

The rag pointed. "Just 'round the corner, there." His mask was a gull with peeling paint.

Butterhill thanked the man and strode on through the puddles. He found the shop crowded between two common houses. It was a low, colorless thing with windows like brittle fog. A bell on the door announced him.

A slight dark-haired man peeked up from a counter, which, like every other inch of the place, was heaped with dusty books. He smiled and said a small hello as the important-looking gentleman marched in, dripping.

"Good afternoon. I am Mr. Butterhill of the Crown House, here on official business," the man said through his mask, "would you happen to be Mr. Pantarbe?"

"Yes," was all the proprietor could manage.

"Very good. It is my understanding that you, sir, are among the finest at deciphering strange symbols and scripts...the best this city has to offer, from what I'm told."

Pantarbe had small worried eyes. "Well, I've been known to dabble in such things..."

"Spare me the modesty. Your writings on the subject are in all the best libraries and your reputation extends far from this bleak little blot of earth. Now then, are you willing to assist me with this matter?"

Before Pantarbe could answer, Butterhill pulled a flat leather box (embossed with a small gold crown) from under his coat and placed it on the counter, bumping a cup of tea.

"Have a look, will you?"

Pantarbe sighed and found his hands trembling when they reached for the box. The lid gave a little creak when he opened it.

"Curious," the pundit said. His expression lightened, then grew intense as he bent close to the piece of paper before him.

Butterhill hovered. "Do you know it?"

"No. Not exactly, I'm afraid. Intriguing... Where did it come from?"

"That's not your concern."

The design was a simple thing, a circle with two characters like imprints from birds' feet, one above and one below.

Pantarbe looked up and smiled timidly. "May I examine this? I should like to check it against my reference materials."

It was just as Butterhill had hoped—a fish can't resist a worm. "Of course. How much time do you think you'll require?"

Pantarbe spoke without removing his eyes from the paper. "I couldn't say, really. A day or so."

Butterhill straightened. "Today is Tuesday; I shall return Thursday first thing. You'll be paid for your time, of course."

The thin, dark-eyed man glanced up. "That's not necessary."

"Thursday then."

The agent turned and marched across the shop. He pushed the door open with the spike of his umbrella and was gone into the rain.

"Good day," Pantarbe called to the closing door.

《《——》》

Darkness had fallen when Pantarbe finished a brief meal at Cutting's Tavern and returned to his shop. It proved a long night full of strong tea and lamp glow. Hour after hour he searched the dusty pages, checking everything from *Long's Dictionary of Cryptography* to *Pepper's Guide to Archaic Symbols*. He found nothing quite like the shapes on the paper.

Half awake at his desk in a corner, Pantarbe heard soft singing out in the street. It had been some time since he had heard any activity, some time since the last carriage had clattered. The lamps had burned low while he had dozed and the windows at the front of the shop were lit more by those outside than those in the room.

The voice grew closer—a voice in the rain—then a shadowy figure drifted up to the glass and seemed to peer in. The singing stopped. Pantarbe swiveled on his stool to get a better view and noticed that the figure, while silhouetted, appeared to be that of a woman. He could just make out the long hair and the wide skirt, but it had to have been a man looking into the shop, for all women were blinded at birth, as was the law.

《《——》》

The rain had ceased and the moon had set by the time Pantarbe made his way home. It was his bath he needed more than sleep—the day just wasn't right without a bath. And so he walked briskly along the cobbled streets puffing warm breath into his owl mask.

Home was in an enormous wooden tenement once painted the color of brick. At this stage in its history, one was forced to wonder if its architect had drawn up his plans while blindfolded, though this was not always the case. The original structure had been added to over the years, many times, in fact, accounting for its many contradictory angles, the multiple gables and incongruous chimneys.

Once inside, the man took a half of a candle from his coat pocket and lit it. The landlord did not provide any sort of lighting in the hallways, nor even on the stairs, of which there were many.

Most of the other tenants were asleep at this hour, but the odd mumbled conversation wept through passing doors and the ancient Mrs. Sugarbrook was tapping her cane like hail. Up four dark flights, Pantarbe found his door and fumbled a key into place.

With the door bolted behind him, Pantarbe started a small fire in his cook stove and put a kettle on. He ran the water in the bath, which was a curtain-partitioned area in his sleep chamber. A blacksmith had fashioned the tub for him after Pantarbe salvaged an old metal barrel from one of the ruined breweries.

"I'm sorry I'm so late, my dear," the bookseller spoke softly into a cage where a small grey and white mouse lived amongst shredded newsprint. Mr. Snowbottom danced around the cage while his master fetched his food.

Pantarbe looked smaller, even more pale than usual without his clothing. He climbed into the warm tub, with hot tea in his favorite tin cup. His body ached from hefting the many heavy old volumes back in the shop. Settled in, his mind went to work.

Back at the university they had called him *The Walking Library*, half out of spite, half out of admiration. More accurately, he was a human card file, for while he did not retain the content of the innumerable books he had read, he knew just where to go to look things up. It only took him a cup of tea and a half-hour in the tub before he figured out where to turn to decipher Butterhill's marking.

《《——》》

There was actually a trace of sunlight in the shop when Pantarbe returned in the morning. The streets were already crowding with gin-breathed merchants who twice a week pushed their heavy carts into The Stain (for there was no proper market). A poultry carriage rattled behind a round donkey, pale dead geese swaying, inverted. Pantarbe could smell the previous night's drink through the slits of the merchant's frog-like mask.

Because market day always brought a few more customers than other days, Pantarbe hustled to make the shop presentable. He hadn't bothered to make order of the mess that the previous night's searching had produced.

Soon the dairy-man was calling from the gutters, "Butter and milk and cream smooth as silk…"

It had come to him in the steam of tea and tub, his own thoughts like a ghost in the head, whispering. He *had* seen something like the symbol that Butterhill brought. The scrap of memory echoed the bird-foot markings and circle —he had seen something along those lines in *Dead Harry's Journal.*

For those unfamiliar, this rare printed item was a collection of coded ramblings that mysteriously appeared in a blank journal when the only person available to pen them was a corpse in an undertaker's cellar. No one, not even Pantarbe had fully deciphered the content, and even then those were the only writings ever to cause him nightmares (outside of Captain Turnkey's unabridged version of *The Church Of Centipedes*).

The book smith knew he owned a copy of the journal, there in his shop, but standing with his hands on his hips, surveying the uneven maze of volumes, he wondered *where*?

《《——》》

Mr. Butterhill, in his office above the South Gardens in the Palace Blocks, received a distressing missive around eight o'clock, Wednesday morning. Balding and bearded without his mask, he hissed at his pipe and marched downstairs to demand that a clandestine force of officers be immediately dispatched to protect Mr. Pantarbe's shop.

《《——》》

The bell on the shop door rang as a customer entered. Pantarbe was knee-deep in books, on the floor in one of the aisles, and could only make out pointed ears jutting up from a mask, moving through one of the other rows.

"Hullo," Pantarbe called, "may I help you in some way?"

A muffled voice called back, "Thank you, no…just browsing."

"Right then."

Pantarbe returned to his scrounging. He felt he was close to finding

Dead Harry's Journal, for a trace of cinnamon touched the air. The book had smelled of cinnamon.

The patron moved slowly, long cape licking at the planks. With a thumb, this shopper flicked open a small hatch at the top of a walking stick; a dial like that on a compass was revealed, its tiny sharp arm twitching.

"Ouch!" Pantarbe knocked his head on a case. A book dropped and he bent to pick it up, spying the feet of the visitor on the other side of the shelf. What small feet, he thought.

"I've got you!"

Pantarbe had found the book and slid it out from under a pile. It was a slim volume of rust-colored leather, and of course there was the smell…like a forgotten holiday exhaling through the dust.

The masked visitor bent over the strange compass as the small metal arm pointed the way. The figure moved more quickly, creaking on the worn floor.

Pantarbe, clutching his prize, headed for his desk in the corner as the customer, a short, caped sort with a long, bony horse-head mask, slipped out the jangling door. The flat leather box that Butterhill had brought him was there on his desk. He flipped it open to have another look, but the paper bearing the symbols was gone.

Moments wasted as Pantarbe lifted the box to look beneath it, then as he searched the floor under the desk. When it occurred to him to go to the door to look after the customer in the oversized mask (who hadn't purchased anything), the figure was gone, lost in the milling shoppers and the merchant carts and the rattling carriages.

A man with a scuffed sage-scented weasel head stepped up to Pantarbe's side. "Excuse me, would you happen to be the shop keep here?"

Pantarbe's small nervous eyes were flicking, distracted. "Yes, yes, what is it?"

"I am Officer Hantarve, of The Crown. Mr. Butterhill has sent me and my men to see to your safety. It has come to our attention that you may be in some degree of danger, I'm sorry to say."

"Danger?"

The weasel looked up and down the street. "Perhaps we should have a word inside."

«« —»»

Without his mask, Hantarve was a darkish man with a great curled mustache. He could not disguise his horror when Pantarbe explained to him that the paper with the symbol had gone missing.

"I had but one customer all morning…a chap in a cape with a pale horse head mask. The mask seemed a bit too large for the body, come to think of it."

Hantarve leaned intimately. "Might it have been a *woman?*"

Pantarbe balked. "Well, I don't see how, I mean it's a difficult enough shop to maneuver through for the sighted, and the person seemed stealthy enough."

"Might it have been a *sighted* woman?"

"Well, the figure was rather small. Very small feet… But how could there be a *sighted* woman?"

Hantarve sighed. "It's a complicated matter."

The bookseller absently fingered the vacant leather box from which the paper had been stolen. "You don't mean to tell me that that was the only copy of the symbol? If that's the case, I could easily recreate it from memory."

"No, no, it's not the only copy. It's just that it might prove troublesome in unsavory hands."

Pantarbe blinked and stared. He wished he were home in his tub with tea and a novel.

"I think it might be best if you return with me to the offices, Mr. Pantarbe."

"But my shop…"

"It's not likely anyone will bother it now."

Reluctance got Pantarbe nowhere. He gathered his mask and *Dead Harry's Journal* and followed the official to the door. Hantarve turned, sniffing and said, "Were you cooking something in here? I smell cinnamon."

«« —»»

Mr. Butterhill sifted his fingers pensively through his beard and studied the curious book that lay open on his desk. Pantarbe sat with hands clenched in lap, gazing at the South Gardens.

"It's so lovely here," Pantarbe noted quietly. "it's many years since I've been to the Crown Blocks."

Butterhill did not look up. "Yes, I've heard all about your esteemed years here and your unfortunate fall from grace. Your misinterpretation of a code saw a few of our spies killed, if memory serves. No bother, old boy, we all make mistakes."

Pantarbe shrank in his seat. "I suppose so," he muttered.

The agent looked up from Dead Harry's scrawlings and poured them both tea. He took his plain, and leaned back in his chair.

"We're in an awful mess, Pantarbe. Something worse than The Great Fire, perhaps even worse than the Green Plague."

That had Pentarbe's attention.

"It is a little known fact that a secretive society of sighted women have been functioning in our good city."

Pantarbe gasped.

"They call themselves The Sisters of the Cyclops." Butterhill snorted a bitter laugh. "Tell me, have you heard of a certain rare coral which when inserted into the skull sockets of the blind can cause sight?"

"Only in rumors, Sir."

"Well, they are more than rumors, I fear. Seems smugglers have been bringing the coral into the city for some months now. A particular band of women secured some of this coral and have since been plotting an event of catastrophic proportions.

"It appears they got in with one of these seance-happy individuals, a Mr. Fibble, who, in his esoteric travels, had secured a certain symbol alleged to have powerful potentialities."

"I've read Fibble. He makes a good case for conjurations and such."

"A terribly good case, yes," Butterhill agreed dourly. "It came to our attention that this outlaw clutch of women were not content to have their vision restored. They were planning to make use of this symbol— the one I took to you—to cause a great deal of havoc. Fibble was prepared to sell it to them for a large sum, you see."

Pantarbe sat like a boy by a grandfather's hearth listening to winter ghost stories. "Remarkable."

"Our men discovered these Sisters of the Cyclops hiding out in a cottage by the West River and sought to stop them before they got their hands on that symbol. We raided them—killed them all, or so, we thought. The conjurer Fibble was there as well, and he was badly wounded in the process. We found the paper with that symbol on Fibble's person and I brought it to you, simply to learn more about it on a precautionary level. But when we interrogated him this morning in the hospital, he informed us that there had been nine women in the gang, yet we had only found the bodies of eight."

"So, one got away?"

Butterhill nodded. "It would seem. It's almost certain that she was wounded, but even so... When we learned that one of the nine was still about, and that several local decoders in the area had turned up dead, I thought it best to send some of my fellows to your shop. A pity they did not arrive sooner."

"So the figure in the horse mask was likely this woman? And she has a hold of the symbol?"

Butterhill nodded.

"What of Fibble? Surely he could tell you more about the symbol than I..." Pantarbe said.

"He was in no condition to communicate, initially, and this morning when we were actually able to speak with him, he did not last long enough to enlighten us more than to say what the thing *might* be used for."

"What might that be?" Pantarbe asked hesitantly.

"According to the late Mr. Fibble, the symbol can be used (in a manner yet to be determined) to bring back to this world all those deceased females, who, under the law, had been blinded in the last five hundred years."

TWO

Ashbrook was painting pictures of the woman a full year before he ever set eyes on her. In tones as sad as sepia, he conjured her, often when he was drunk or half asleep, always when rain was at the windows.

She was long, with hair like a pour of rusty water, and a shabby grey dress. She was beautiful in the way that a November wood was beautiful, or an abandoned building, dusted and lonely in Midwinter.

Sometimes he painted her standing against birches, as if she were an emanation of the trees. Other times she was propped against shadows, her wearied features hinted by candlelight.

In the evening, down in The Stain, when the artist was staggering home through the alleys, he saw the woman from behind—the rusty hair running down her grey shoulders. She slipped into the doorway of an abandoned mill and was gone into the blackness.

"Wait," Young Ashbrook called. He ran after her, though the drink was in his legs.

Dusk did little to illustrate the mill's interior. The place was a smell as much as a sight, as if The Great Fire had burned the very air of the place, those years ago. The brick walls were blackened like a smoke oven, and scorched beams crossed above in a haze of webs.

Weak footsteps sounded somewhere in the mill.

"Hullo!" Ashbrook called. His voice flew off and faded.

It was too late for sunlight and too early for street lamps, thus the windows provided only so much illumination. Still, it was enough to allow Ashbrook to maneuver through the various chambers.

Leaves had stolen in from the broken windows and he could hear the woman's skirt hissing through them as she moved ahead. Some of the furnishings had survived the blaze, table tops like coffin lids and charred chairs crumpled in upon themselves like great dead insects. There were plenty of things to trip over, yet the woman was steady about her course and Ashbrook caught glimpses as she sailed through the shadows, her hair and skirts just brushed by the light from the windows. She was swift for a blind woman, he thought as he stumbled behind.

The man lost track of the woman after a time and he paused to collect himself. The voices out in the street seemed very far away and momentarily he heard the floor above him creak.

"Ah!"

He found the stairs. They were littered with ash and bits of broken glass that crunched like ice. Drunk as he was, he managed to make it to the top, his mask filled with the smell of ale. He stood in a vast, open room, empty but for a circle of figures at the center.

Ashbrook hesitated. "What's this then?" he muttered.

None of the figures spoke, nor even turned to acknowledge him.

Resisting the sudden urge to turn and go back down the stairs, Ashbrook took a step forward.

"Uh, hullo…" he said softly.

There was no reply but for that of the groaning floor. Ashbrook moved closer, wobbling and squinting.

"I do hope I'm not disturbing anything…"

No movement or sound came from the figures, but Ashbrook could make out more as he crossed the first half of the great chamber. Blackened chair legs had been placed at opposite ends of the circle—they looked like a giant bird's feet.

Dizzy from the chase, Ashbrook tottered up to the back of the nearest person and put a hand on its shoulder. The figure fell forward, the loosely draped clothing spilling away from an understructure of wood and wire. The thing clattered on the floor.

"My word!" the man drew back. "What's this?"

His eyes focused in the gloom. The other figures appeared to be effigies as well, their heads mere bundles of twine and cloth, the hands only worn gloves, the torsos salvaged from bits of ruined mill equipment. What was most curious about these figures was the fact that his likeness had been crudely rendered in dull red paint upon their cloth faces; his own blurry features stared back.

One of the figures stepped forward, and in the weak light he saw that this one was different from the rest. It was the woman from his paintings. She was tall and thin and her rusty hair hung slack across her shoulders. A pale hand hid the left side of her face.

"Hullo," Ashbrook said cautiously.

The woman stopped at the center of the circle and took away her mask of fingers. A sickly glow was revealed, the piece of polished coral like a coin of moonlight over one eye.

Ashbrook, never having been seen by a woman in all his twenty-five years, shuddered.

A soft voice fell on him like snow scattered on a field. "I have dreamed of you each night for a year."

"You…you can *see* me?"

"Yes, but don't let that frighten you. I would never have known how truly beautiful you are if I had never had this chance to gaze upon you."

Ashbrook took a cautious step toward the center. "I have dreamed you, as well…"

The woman reached up and worked the buttons at the neck of her dress. Her hands crawled down her front like spiders and the garment fell open between her breasts. Ashbrook's eyes moved down to the bare belly and he noticed that it had two navels, one above the other. The lower one was larger and wet with blood.

She floated to him and crushed a piece of paper into his hand, her gaunt face close, half illuminated. Then she pressed her body against him and brushed his ear with her small mouth. She told him what she needed him to do, and once the whisper was finished, she slid down him, painting with her blood.

Ashbrook uncrumpled the paper and stared down at it as the woman died on the floor.

THREE

"Let's get you some garments that don't reek of old books, or we'll have my wife sneezing herself bald," Butterhill said to Pantarbe.

The Crown official had insisted that the bookseller return home with him for the time being, as a matter of safety. Pantarbe was only half-comfortable with the idea. He was not the most social of creatures, for one, and he would likely feel out of place around people of position, though he was warming to Butterhill, ever so slightly.

But, Pantarbe concluded, it might be wise to stay somewhere safer than his flat. That disguised woman had found him easily enough, after all, and she had killed several other decipherers already.

Walking to Butterhill's handsome black carriage, Pantarbe had a question for the taller man. "Wouldn't you think the woman would have attacked me in the shop this morning if she meant me a harm?"

Butterhill huffed, "Who can know a woman's mind? Especially these criminal types? Perhaps she'd spotted my men snooping about outside and was in too great a hurry. You're a lucky fellow to be alive at any rate."

The coach was comfortably lined with red velvet, and the suspended cab took the bumps well. The driver brought them to an expensive shop where Butterhill was known to the tailor. Butterhill and the proprietor picked out several outfits for the mild bookseller.

Pantarbe's head poked out from behind a dressing curtain as Butterhill sat puffing his pipe and tapping his foot.

"I'm not sure I quite feel myself," Pantarbe muttered.

"Here now! Step out and let's have a look," Butterhill ordered.

Pantarbe shuffled out in his new suit (and pinching shoes) and stood awkwardly.

The tailor was around him like a moth. "Ahhh, a fine fit. Dashing!"

Butterhill worried his beard. "Mm. Not bad. Right then, we'll take these and the others, but we'll be needing a new mask, as well."

From the tailor's shop they rode up Winningston to one of the best mask purveyors in the city. The shop smelled of the many herbs that were used to scent the masks, and rows of creatures stared from shelves as if the men were in a zoo of severed heads.

Butterhill was admiring a rather unhappy looking gargoyle-faced item, but Pantarbe was holding out for a bird.

"I'm rather fond of owls, actually," he protested meekly.

Butterhill yielded and turned to the shop owner. "Find him a bloody owl."

"Nothing too stern," Pantarbe called after the man.

Several owls later, the right thing was found. It was slightly smaller than Pantarbe's battered old headgear. The new full-head mask was honey-colored, subtly brushed with a suggestion of feathers. The beak poked out an inch or so and the eye openings were tastefully disguised. There was a pleasing nutmeg smell to the whole.

"Well," Butterhill said, "do you like it?"

"Oh, yes, very much. Thank you, Mr. Butterhill."

"Very good. Then let's be off."

Pantarbe hesitated. "There's just one thing…"

"What might that be?"

"I'd rather not leave my mouse at the flat, you see, and I was wondering if I might bring him along?"

Butterhill sighed. "Give me your key and I'll send someone to fetch it."

"Oh, thank you. He's never spent a night alone before."

Butterhill slipped his dark animal head on and mumbled, "Mouse."

««——»»

When Pantarbe was a small boy, he thought that the fireplace could ward off any nasty menace that his imagination might conjure. Sitting by the logs in the Butterhill parlor, he found himself envying that distant simplicity. But then he had put off opening *Dead Harry's Journal* long enough.

A portrait of one of the Butterhills' sons hung above the mantel. It showed the boy in the fashionable style, the legs disproportionately short, and the stylized head a bit too large. In the painting the boy was dressed in his best suit with a puppy at his feet and a fox mask under his arm.

There were other portraits as well, throughout the impressive house, more of the sons than of the daughters, though Pantarbe had found the little blind girls more charming at the dinner table.

Mrs. Butterhill had proved pleasant. She had talked to him about books and professed a love of music and imported spices. Mr. Butterhill had occupied himself by grumbling at the servants.

Now, with the noisy little boys off in their noisy little dreams, and the house quiet but for the snapping of the logs, Pantarbe opened the slim leather book and went about his task.

«« —»»

Dead Harry had a style all his own.
THE FIRST NIGHT I AM IN A GROVE OF WILLOWS
THE NIGHT IS LIKE SLEEP
THERE IS NO MOON, BUT I SEE
I HEAR OTHERS LIKE ME
EVERYWHERE

That was the first passage and it still gave Pantarbe chills to read, even after all these years. It had proved the easiest to decipher too, for as the journal progressed Harry's code modified, became more complex, integrating dead languages, numbers and prehistoric hieroglyphics. Pantarbe would be needing to return to his shop to get some of his reference books if he were to tackle some of the later installments.

Pantarbe looked down to the cage at his feet where Mr. Snowbottom slept safely in his tattered bed of newspaper. The man smiled fondly. Sleep wasn't such a bad idea, he thought, closing the book. It had been quite a day.

178

FOUR

Weeds had found the tower long before Ashbrook did—the garden was a brittle jungle of them, their redeeming wildflowers gone with the summer. There was the odd bird-neglected berry and cheerless rose hips like shriveled nipples.

The structure was an oddity there in The Narrows, where working class families crowded into tall, thin tenements the color of salt (with plain green trim). Built in the time of Morris the Third, it was a high cylindrical thing, an anomaly, its brickwork the dark of fruitcake. It might as well have been built of old fruitcake, for it was as moldy as they come—even the wooden, tall-windowed chamber that capped the thing was prone to lichens and grey-green splotches of damp color.

Ashbrook didn't need a key to get in; the door was unlocked and the layered rust on the handle left flecks like cinnamon on his palm. He wiped his hand on his leg, removed his salamander mask, set it on the floor, and started up the spiral of stairs using the coral eye of the dead woman as a light. The soft blue glow illuminated the veined plaster walls and the metal grate steps, of which there seemed an inexhaustible supply.

He paused halfway up, not used to this sort of exertion, and, catching his breath, heard a dull thump somewhere in the dark above. While there was a hollow quality to the noise, it did not sound the way feet did on the metal stairs. The thump came again, reverberating slightly.

No matter. Ashbrook proceeded, the crinkled paper bearing the symbol still in his pocket. Up he went, higher and higher, scabs of rust (loosed by his feet) clattering in the void below. The blue thing glowing in his hand was like the ghost of a firefly.

When at last he came to the chamber at the top of the building, he was clammy with sweat and breathing hard. He braced himself in the doorway and stared in at a circular claw-foot tub, its calcium pallor stark, defined by the light of the multiple windows that ringed the room.

A thump, a pause and a thump came from the tub. Ashbrook took a step forward and peered in. An unpainted cylindrical mask floated face-down in old grey water. It was a full-head mask, as was common to the century, and in its water-suspended state it occasionally bumped up against the side of the tub. Thump.

Remembering the rusty-haired woman's whispered instructions, he took out the ball of paper and straightened it. The paper showed a symbol: a circle between markings like inked bird-prints. Ashbrook poked two fingers through the center of the circle, making a ragged hole in the paper.

After a moment of hesitation, he reached for the mask and lifted it from the tub. He held it like a puppet in one hand and held the punctured paper against his face with the other. He kissed the mask's hard lips through the hole. Then, though it was dripping and cold and stank of drowned cinnamon, he placed the mask over his head.

Ashbrook saw his reflection in the water. He had never seen a mask that had a human face before. The features were understated, primitive even, but human, nonetheless, even feminine, some might say, though a *female* mask with eye-holes would strike most as incongruous.

The coral eye slipped from the man's fingers and plopped into the grey water. It sank to the bottom where it shone like a moon through clouds.

Many rituals favor a sacrifice (consensual or not) and so, inexplicably, Ashbrook found himself diving through the glass in one of the windows. The mask was full of screams on the way down, but young Ashbrook could not tell if they were his own, or those of voices that lived in the mask.

FIVE

A coach carrying Pantarbe, Butterhill and an armed Sgt. Belfry entered The Stain at the onset of evening. They rode along Thornbridge with its many warehouses and poorly disguised "sleep parlors" where destitute women, with no other means of sustenance, entertained on grey mattresses between drab cloth partitions. Butterhill scowled at gravitating (respectably dressed) gentlemen.

Their destination was Pantarbe's bookshop. The journey had been at his request; he needed to gather some reference materials to help him in deciphering *Dead Harry's journal*.

Butterhill waited in the coach, scrounging the last bowl of tobacco from his pouch while the other two went inside. Pantarbe was sad to find his shop feeling so abandoned, and were it not for the stern, hovering Sgt. Belfry, he would have reassured the place aloud.

Eventually the two reappeared and lugged armfuls of books to the rear storage compartment of the coach. The sun was all but set and the shadows both lengthened and darkened; one was given the impression that they were generated by the miserable buildings themselves. Rather than showing *against* the worn street cobbles, the shadows seemed to seep up from between the stones.

The party returned to a better part of the city and stopped at Butterhill's request. He needed to replenish his supply of tobacco. This time it was Belfry who waited in the carriage; he contented himself with one of those disreputable little weeklies that catered to sensationalism and favored covers depicting women being menaced. His fullhead mask was on the shelf above his head, for while masks were required in the street, this demand was spared those aboard closed-in vehicles. Pantarbe got out to stretch his legs and peer into shop windows.

There was a certain imported coral, made available to those who could afford it, which possessed a strange green luminosity. Longerlasting than any candle, and reliable in the draftiest situation, it was as desirable for its functionality as it was as a mark of status. Fortunately for the suppliers of the stuff, the coral's glow did not last indefinitely.

It was the unearthly radiance of such coral that met Butterhill when he entered the small foyer of the building that housed the tobacconist. He closed the door to the street and noticed a table that held a glass lantern containing small green pebbles. Half brightened by this were three young girls seated in a row on a wooden settle, their six small feet dangling above the floor. The impression was not a pleasant one, for the sickly light made it look as if the girls were sitting underwater, this observation reinforced by the fact that each had damp dark hair on the shoulders, as if the trio had just been dragged from some lake. At least their dresses were pretty.

Inexplicably uncomfortable, Butterhill hastened to the inner door, eager to be free of their empty stares and odd little smiles.

"Good evening, Sir," the tobacconist greeted him, smiling broadly from behind his counter when Butterhill entered the shop proper.

The shop was worn and warm, the high flames in the fireplace snapping like a flag in a tempest. The agent of the Crown stopped in the doorway just to breathe the place in.

"Good evening," he returned to the owner, who was as pleasant a man as one could hope to meet.

"What will it be this evening, Sir?"

Butterhill approached a rack where there were rows of jars filled with dark, shredded tobacco. He let his nose direct him and peeked under a number of lids to get a better sense of the particulars.

"I'm not quite certain, to be truthful," Butterhill said, sniffing expertly.

Outside the fog had come on and the lamp-lighters were busy with the street lanterns. Waiting for his friend, Pantarbe gazed into this and that store window. Pedestrians were rendered as smudges in the dusky gloom and moved peculiarly, as if the heavy air slowed their progress.

Admiring a display of small ceramic animals, Pantarbe was only half aware of those around him. A figure floated up from behind, like a ghost in the glass, the eyes of its fish-head helmet as big as tea saucers. This person hovered momentarily over his shoulder and only drifted away when Pantarbe turned to have a better look. He glanced as the figure departed, saw thin breeches-legs poking down from under a gentleman's great coat. The coat actually looked a bit too large for the wearer.

Back in the cozy shop, we rejoin Butterhill, who was close to a purchase. He had narrowed his choices down to two...one with a scent like August and orange rind, which was a favored scent so far as his wife was concerned, and the other a rich North Country blend with a touch of apple that reminded him of his first childhood mask. He decided on the first, for the sake of his missus.

Waiting while the tobacconist wielded his scoop, Butterhill turned to the door behind him, having heard the suggestion of giggles coming from the other side. Perhaps it was only pigeons out in the street. At any rate, the shop keep seemed not to notice, but then there were distracting noises to consider... The poorly seasoned firewood was hissing like a pail of snakes, and the logs were popping, their sparks hopping out like incandescing crickets.

The transaction was completed (with a healthy tip) and Butterhill turned to leave. Going out the door, he made the obligatory, if inaccurate observation, "Your three daughters are lovely."

With the door closed behind him, Butterhill did not hear the tobacconist say, "Daughters? I have no daughters."

《《——》》

Exiting the shop, the Crown agent immediately saw a man in an owl-head mask crumpled on the cobbles by the coach. The door to the cab hung open and the driver stood dumbfounded.

"Pantarbe!"

Butterhill rushed to his friend and knelt, putting a hand on him. He looked up at the masked driver for an explanation.

"I don't know what happened, Mr. Butterhill. I was occupied but a moment, adjusting the harnesses, and when I came back I found *this*…"

The bookseller stirred, groaned and pointed to the carriage; he muttered, "I've fainted, I think."

Exasperated by his fright, Butterhill stood and only then noticed what it was that made Pantarbe swoon. Sgt. Belfry was slumped in the cab—it looked as if he had been doused with beet juice—a kitchen knife had been pushed deeply into one of his eye sockets.

SIX

Mrs. Butterhill moved slowly into the study where Pantarbe hunched over a clutter of open books. She turned her lovely face in his direction—she was impassive, inscrutable as a mask. He had found that she always knew when he was about—she could smell the vague nutmeg impression that his mask left on his person. He had wondered in the past if the tradition of scenting the masks had come about as a way for women to identify individuals to some degree.

"Forgive me if I interrupt, Mr. Pantarbe."

"No need for apology, Mrs. Butterhill—this is your house, after all." He very briefly considered adding that her interruptions were welcome ones, but it was not in his nature to flirt, most especially not with the wife of a friend. What he lacked in boldness he made up for with integrity, or so he liked to think.

Mrs. Butterhill exhibited the restraint and gentle grace that her sex and position demanded, that society demanded. She moved quietly to the window and listened for the activity of carriages below in the street.

"There are hundreds dead, my husband tells me," the woman said.

"Yes, hundreds, perhaps many more that we don't know of. It's the most terrible thing."

"All of those killed are men, I understand."

"So far as we know, yes."

It had only taken a matter of days before the Crown House placed the city under martial law. A severe curfew was in effect and some in power had even suggested that mask wearing be forbidden on the street, so that the returning dead could not disguise themselves with masks, but the doctrines of the church were staunchly set against the notion. There were, after all, laws forbidding public unmasking.

"In a strange way…" Mrs. Butterhill started, but then thought better of it and went silent.

Pantarbe studied her and pressed, "Yes?"

The woman turned to face him with her appealing, useless eyes. "While this horror cannot be condoned, is there not some element of inevitability about it? For five hundred years man has seen fit to take away the very eyes that nature bestowed upon women… There was bound to be some sort of consequence, eventually."

Pantarbe stiffened. "Umm, yes, I suppose you're right to say. I hadn't thought of it, myself, but of course you're right."

"I have imagined all my life what it would be like to see. I would have given up my hands and my speech and my ears to spend a day sighted."

Pantarbe stared at her, at how beautiful she was, even with her features weighted in sadness. He could not imagine *not* seeing her, or anything else for that matter. Men had sight and women did not, that was simply the way of things. Usually he was immune to the concept; still, he found himself thinking that he would have, at that moment, taken one of his eyes and given it to Mrs. Butterhill, if there were indeed a way.

"Is it not true, Mr. Pantarbe, that these women whom have come back are sighted in death?"

"It would seem so."

"How terribly strange. As much as I have dreamed of sight, I'm not about to die for the privilege."

"I should hope not!"

"…and so I wish you the best in finding a way to bring an end to this situation, Mr. Pantarbe, for I do not wish to return from my rest as one of these sad, murderous creatures. Besides, it has always brought

184

me comfort to believe that once I have passed from this world of words and laws, I will be delivered to a freer realm where I shall be rewarded the vision I was not allowed here."

Pantarbe said, "I hope you're right, Mrs. Butterhill."

The woman excused herself and drifted from the room, the hem of her wide skirt sighing across the floor. Pantarbe turned back to his work. He had progressed in making sense of the previously undeciphered installments of *Dead Harry's Journal*. The circle in the center of the mysterious symbol in question stared up at him like the eye of a cyclops.

«« — »»

Once a year a migration of tiny silvery birds no bigger than bumblebees passed above the midnight city. In every other year the residents had turned out to watch the icy stream of the things as it glittered above the dark buildings, but this year the audience only peered from windows, as the streets were in the hands of the military.

Still, in the morning, the soft little feathers were scattered on the cobblestones like a dusting of frost, or the miniaturized ghosts of autumn leaves.

Mr. Butterhill, in his sleeplessness, had heard the strange cries echoing above the city as he lay in his bed, cursing himself for failing to stop the ritual that had summoned the dead women. A similar guilt was plaguing Pantarbe. Both appeared in need of sleep that morning in the offices above the bleak South Gardens of the Palace Blocks.

The Crown agent was just finishing up with a reporting officer, who said, "While we don't seem capable of *killing* these creatures, they can be made ineffective through dismantling."

"Thank you, Captain."

The officer was dismissed and Butterhill hastily made out an order for large quantities of burning oil with which to destroy the restless remains of the largely incapacitated women. It had come to his ears that great mounds of gibbering heads and fluttery hands were being gathered by the army as they progressed in thinning the horrid ranks of returnees. While there were no reports of severed limbs actually causing any harm, the risk was not worth taking.

He also ordered the metal shops to turn out an emergency quantity of the large chopping knives so common among the colonists in the jungled South Islands. That business tended, he turned to Pantarbe.

His friend was standing by the window looking out upon the seemingly deserted city—the Palace Blocks were more fortress-like than ever. The sky was like a skim of pond ice above while below a dusting of silvery feathers borrowed the shape of breezes.

"What's this good news I hear of, Pantarbe?"

The bookseller broke from his musing and went to sit at the front of Butterhill's impressive desk.

"Well, I think I may have uncovered something of worth. In the section where Dead Harry goes on about the varied ways of summoning back the dead, he appears to provide maps to locations that are best suited to that purpose. The mystical character that has been at the heart of this matter, it turns out, is as much a map as it is a power symbol."

Butterhill sat forward.

"Once I determined this, I examined a map of the city's streets and I found *this*…"

Pantarbe placed a map before his friend. He had marked a certain spot in colored ink. It showed an unconventional intersection of streets.

"What is this circle in the center?" Butterhill asked, pointing.

"It would appear to be some sort of building."

The circular building was the joining point for a number of small side streets, which seen from above resembled two opposite imprints that might have been left by an enormous bird.

"Fine work, Pantarbe! Didn't I know all along that you would figure this thing out? What now?"

"Well, there are several rituals one might apply to deactivate a summoning. I'm afraid I must go to the place on this map and try my hand." Pantarbe looked very glum about this prospect.

"Right then."

Butterhill opened a drawer and fished out two silvery revolvers. He placed one on the desk. "Are you familiar with these contraptions?"

Pantarbe shrank visually. "Umm, I'm afraid not."

"It's quite simple, really. You hold it *here*, you point *this*, and you squeeze *that*."

Pantarbe picked the alien thing up as gingerly as he would his beloved pet mouse.

SEVEN

The low air was black and wretched with the smoke of burning body parts, while above, nature's solemn clouds lumbered. The Stain was more dismal than usual, its abandoned streets paved a ghostly silver where feathers had fallen.

From the windows of their coach, Pantarbe and Butterhill observed soldiers about the unpleasant business of carrying dead men from the many buildings, heaping them onto produce wagons. Others, armed with large brush-chopping blades, loaded carts with the broken, not entirely inactive remains of dead women.

A cylindrical tower poked up from The Narrows where several tight streets converged. It was a dark thing of moldy brick, which, upon closer inspection, was settled in a garden of weeds. A rotting wooden chamber with tall windows capped the thing. Pantarbe glimpsed a figure up there, through broken panes.

A team of the Crown's best had secured the old tower and stood about in the weeds that made its moat. Each wore the grey coat and full-head wolf mask that was standard issue at the time.

Butterhill climbed out first and saluted the men.

"Everything in order here?"

An officer—as denoted by the darker cast of his mask—gave a muffled reply. "Yes, Sir."

"Right."

Butterhill led the way, with Pantarbe behind him and the two guards that had ridden with them in tow. There was nothing much but echoes in the dim cylinder's interior, only wrinkled plaster walls and an upward spiral of rusty grate steps. The men began clanking up, sprinkles of dislodged rust raining into the dark below.

The four men were halfway up when the sound of gunfire rang outside. The two guards charged back down, struggling to unshoulder their rifles as they went. Butterhill hesitated. More shots sounded.

"Stay right here, Pantarbe," Butterhill ordered, then he too descended.

While the Crown agent clattered down out of view, Pantarbe moved higher on the stairs. The small pouch containing the herbs and scripts he would need for his ritual bounced against his leg.

Higher still, Pantarbe saw the doorway that led into the top chamber. A strange blue light issued from within, and, as he progressed even further, he became aware of a certain noise, like a person's weight shifting on ice or more probably, bits of glass beneath a boot.

«« — »»

Butterhill reached the ground level only moments after his two guards—they were the first things he saw when he thrust out of the building. Both men lay face-down in the weeds alongside the felled driver, with dark exit wounds staining the backs of their coats.

A half-moon formation of wolf-masked soldiers stood around the doorway of the tower. Earlier, in his haste, he had not noticed how their helmets sat too low on their shoulders, or how their jackets fell too far on their skinny legs.

"Good God!"

Butterhill turned as quickly as he could, even as the figures raised their rifles in unison. He charged up the first few stairs while a thundering volley shook the tower. Projectiles clanged loudly against the metal steps and punched jagged mouths in the plaster.

«« — »»

Pantarbe was all but panting when he reached the top chamber. The booming of guns came from the garden and desperate steps pounded on the stairs behind him. Terrified, he faced the lone masked soldier that stood by a circular claw-foot bathing tub.

"What's happening?" he cried.

The soldier's wolf face was glazed with an impassive blue that radiated from the rancid tub water. It was a serene color, like the blue of dusk snow.

The figure said nothing, though it took a step toward him.

"What's going on out there?" Pantarbe insisted.

He stepped aside as if to let the soldier pass, for the blued figure came closer. More shots banged, this time from within the tower well.

In a motion that seemed a blur, the soldier swung a wide-bladed chopper that made a terrible splitting sound as it struck Pantarbe in the top of his owl mask.

The man collapsed, the blade buried in his helmet. He fell face-first into the tub of old water, his ribs striking the edge hard. Through his eye slits he saw a single blue circle of coral staring at him from the bottom of the tub.

Pantarbe groaned, his mouth and mask full of the tub's dark contents, and shoved himself back. He fumbled for the weapon that Butterhill had given him, while the thing in soldier's garb unsheathed a cruel bayonet and came to meet him.

Before Pantarbe could take action, shots rang out and the soldier jerked with impacts. Butterhill appeared in the doorway, his pistol trailing smoke. When the figure did not go down, he held the sidearm out and fired again. This time the bullets struck high and the wolf head was kicked from its wearer.

Pantarbe only caught a glimpse of the thing as it toppled back against one of the windows. The face was all the more ghastly for the blue luminescence of the room—framed in a spill of dank dark hair, it was a rough sculpture of bone and soot, the small eyes staring, seeing.

The woman smashed through the window and fell without a scream. They heard her thump in the weeds below.

Pantarbe tore off his mask—the blade still embedded. The edge had only just creased his flesh, hardly enough to draw blood.

Butterhill was breathless. "Do what you must do and do it swiftly, Pantarbe. There are more of them below."

The Crown man reloaded his own pistol and took Pantarbe's as well. Positioned at the top of the stairs, he held the ascending guisers off while Pantarbe followed one of Dead Harry's recipes.

The book smith plucked that glowing blue disc from the tub then set about sprinkling his herbs and drawing symbols in the water. All the while the room shook with Butterhill's gunfire and approaching steps sounded on the stairs.

When there were no more herbs to scatter and no more magic words to speak, Pantarbe knelt back and watched as the grey water lightened. A soft mist rose on the surface and then an eerie cry seemed to rise from everywhere in The Narrows. It came from the near tenements and the shaded alleys between them. It sounded from the empty streets of The Stain, and beyond, as if the entire city were some great dying gull.

He saw from the window as the women dressed in dead soldiers' clothes sagged to the ground. He heard the others toppling listlessly down the stairs, their rifles clattering as they fell. Five hundred years' worth of resurrected women were dead once again.

EIGHT

In the morning Pantarbe gathered his things and prepared to leave the fine Butterhill residence for his place in The Stain. He packed his books and reference papers and, carrying his cage down the great stairs, spoke to his mouse, "We're going home, Mr. Snowbottom."

While Mr. Butterhill, who insisted on purchasing Pantarbe a new owl mask, waited outside in his carriage, Mrs. Butterhill waited at the door to see him off (in so many words.)

The woman offered her hand. "We will miss you, Mr. Pantarbe," she said kindly.

"And I you," Panatarbe managed, shy even in his invisibility, "thank you for the generous hospitality of which I have been shown."

"It was our pleasure. You must come visit sometime." (People who never saw each other again always said things like that.)

Pantarbe smiled. "Yes, I'd like to, I'm sure."

Without releasing the woman's hand, Pantarbe turned it over and placed something small into the palm.

"A small gift," he said, smiling as she closed her fingers around the luminous blue coral disc. "It's simple to use...you merely place it over one eye."

Scott Thomas is the author of *Westermead*, *Cobwebs and Whispers* and *Shadows of Flesh*. He is the co-author of *Punktown: Shades of Grey* along with his brother Jeffrey Thomas. His fiction has appeared in a number of anthologies which include: *The Year's Best Fantasy and Horror #15*, *The Year's Best Horror #22*, *Leviathan 3*, *Punktown: Third Eye*, *Deathrealms* and *The Ghost in the Gazebo*.

Thomas lives in Maine.

30922555R00119

Made in the USA
San Bernardino, CA
26 February 2016